Touch of the
Black Widow

Also by Bea Carlton
in Large Print:

Deadly Gypsy Blue
In the Foxes' Lair
In the House of the Enemy
Moonshell
Voices from the Mist

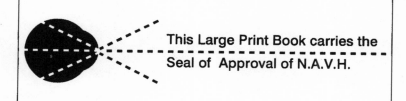

Touch of the Black Widow

Bea Carlton

Thorndike Press • Waterville, Maine

Sequel to The Secret of Windthorn

Published in 2004 by arrangement with Bea Carlton.

Thorndike Press® Large Print Christian Mystery.

The tree indicium is a trademark of Thorndike Press.

The text of this Large Print edition is unabridged.
Other aspects of the book may vary from the original edition.

Set in 16 pt. Plantin by Al Chase.

Printed in the United States on permanent paper.

Library of Congress Cataloging-in-Publication Data

Carlton, Bea.
    Touch of the black widow / Bea Carlton.
      p. cm.
    Sequel to: The secret of Windthorn.
    ISBN 0-7862-5706-7 (lg. print : hc : alk. paper)
    1. Mexico City (Mexico) — Fiction.   2. Large type books.
I. Title.
PS3553.A736T68 2004
813′.54—dc21   2003054242

Dedicated with love and appreciation
to
Lois and Bill Carpenter,
missionaries to Mexico,
for opening your home and hearts to me.

As the Founder/CEO of NAVH, the only national health agency solely devoted to those who, although not totally blind, have an eye disease which could lead to serious visual impairment, I am pleased to recognize Thorndike Press* as one of the leading publishers in the large print field.

Founded in 1954 in San Francisco to prepare large print textbooks for partially seeing children, NAVH became the pioneer and standard setting agency in the preparation of large type.

Today, those publishers who meet our standards carry the prestigious "Seal of Approval" indicating high quality large print. We are delighted that Thorndike Press is one of the publishers whose titles meet these standards. We are also pleased to recognize the significant contribution Thorndike Press is making in this important and growing field.

Lorraine H. Marchi, L.H.D.
Founder/CEO
NAVH

* Thorndike Press encompasses the following imprints: Thorndike, Wheeler, Walker and Large Print Press.

1

Max Parrish strolled down the winding path toward the fountain in the center of the large enclosed patio. His merry whistle complemented the brilliant Mexico City sun as it glinted on his tawny hair. A scar running from his right eyebrow up into his hairline made a vivid slash of red on his face.

The whistle died abruptly on his lips. He shaded his amber eyes with one hand to peer through the bars of the high wrought-iron dividing fence that separated his employer's patio from the neighbor's.

A woman lay head down on the steps of a palm-thatched gazebo. Her body was limp and lifeless, like a life-sized doll tossed down on the steps. The head rested on the lower step; her legs above, extended out onto the floor of the open-sided *ramada*. The late spring sun, glistening in her dark red hair spilling out over the ground, shone full into her pale ivory face and closed eyelids.

Max's heart lurched and began to thud against his rib cage. He crossed to the large gate in a few quick bounds and yanked futilely at the heavy iron gate; a large locked padlock hung on the door.

"Miss, can you hear me?" he called urgently, but the lifeless figure didn't move.

"Hello, in there! Can anyone hear me?" He shouted loudly through the vertical bars. "There's a lady in there who needs help!"

Max could dimly hear the sounds of the Mexico City traffic in the streets outside the walls of the hacienda but nothing else.

"The phone! I'll call the police!" Max whirled and almost collided with Jorge, the wiry little Mexican gardener.

"Is something wrong?" Jorge asked in Spanish, a quizzical expression on his weathered brown face.

"Can you get this gate open?" Max asked brusquely in his halting Spanish.

"*Si, Si,*" Jorge said, and obligingly pulled a large key from his pocket, inserting it into the padlock.

The gate swung open and Max rushed forward, with Jorge limping behind. Kneeling beside the slim, still body of the young woman, Max wondered with mounting horror if she was dead. Then his blunt, probing fingers found a pulse. He was trying to decide whether to risk lowering her from her awkward position on the steps when the woman's eyes opened.

Narrowed against the glare of the sun, her eyes searched his face. Max felt his face grow hot under the scrutiny of those clear grey eyes — feathered into blue at the edges — and framed in thick, dark lashes.

Then the girl stirred and raised one hand weakly, brushing it across her eyes before struggling to rise, awkwardly because of her head-down position on the steps.

Max moved quickly to assist her, almost lifting her from the steps. He set her upright on the lowest step of the gazebo where she swayed and would have fallen had he not held her.

She was tall for a woman, but Max was amazed at how light she was. Shockingly thin and fragile. But in spite of her almost emaciated condition, she was the most beautiful woman he had ever seen. High cheekbones in a delicately carved oval face, slim shapely arms and hands. And her hair was a rare shade of glowing russet-red. Even in her almost helpless state, her bearing was unconsciously regal.

"Are you all right?" Max asked.

"I-I think so. C-could you help me to a-a chair?" The voice was scarcely more than a whisper.

"Hold on to me," Max directed. As Jorge

limped back to his work, Max helped the woman up.

Moving as if her legs were weighted and uncooperative, she clung tightly to Max's arm as he helped her to a lawn chair under a shade tree. She more fell than sat down in it. Laying her head back wearily, she closed her eyes as if it were too great an effort to keep them open.

Watching her anxiously, Max asked, "Can I get a doctor or someone to help you?"

"No! Please don't call anyone!" Her eyes opened wide with alarm as she implored, "They'll make me come in if they know. I-I'll be better right away. I must have passed out."

She pressed an unsteady hand over her eyes for a moment before making an effort to sit upright. A sound came from her lips that was meant to be a light laugh, he knew, but it came off poorly. "I do that rather often — pass out, I mean — so it isn't anything to be alarmed about."

She drew in a shaky breath. "See, I'm getting stronger already."

Taking another deep breath, she settled back against the chair, resting her head on the chair back. Her pale lips curved into a slight smile. "I'm Autumn Caldwell. Thank you so much for coming to my aid. I'm glad you found me instead of *them*."

Max had difficulty speaking. Always shy around women, he now found himself almost speechless in the presence of this goddess-like beauty. He was acutely aware of his own hulking homeliness and had to swallow twice before any words would come.

"I-I'm Max P-Parrish," he stuttered and dropped his eyes in confusion. He knew his face was flaming red. "I-I'm the chauffeur and personal assistant for Skye and Joy Windthorn next door."

Suddenly, his cherished job sounded lowly and unimportant even to his own ears, and he just wanted to get back into his own safe domain. His gravelly voice sounded abrupt and gruff, "If you're okay, I'll get on back." He turned away.

Autumn's soft voice stopped him. "Please don't go, Max."

Surprised, Max turned back to face her.

There was nothing of the coquette in Autumn's face as her grey-blue eyes looked up into his. Her voice was beseeching and a slight flush colored her pale cheeks. "I'm so lonely I could die! They won't let anyone come to see me anymore so it is heaven to be able to talk to anyone besides them.

11

Couldn't you sit down and talk a bit?"

Her almost childlike sincerity melted Max's diffidence. He lowered himself into a lawn chair near her. "The Windthorns are away for the day, so I'm not in a hurry," he said. "Could I get you something to drink? You look awfully pale."

"Oh, would you? And you must join me. There's some coffee, juice, and rolls over on the table in the gazebo. Juana, our maid, brought them out a few minutes ago. There are even extra cups and glasses, in case the rest of the family came out here for breakfast."

Max brought the food — still on a tray — and set in on a small table by Autumn's chair.

"Let me pour," Autumn said. "Would you like some coffee? And these yeast rolls are delicious. Our cook makes them."

Max accepted coffee and a roll as Autumn said conversationally, "Your employers — Skye and Joy Windthorn — are they vacationing here in Mexico?"

Max's yellow eyes glowed as he said with pride, "No, Mr. Windthorn is an archaeologist, and he's on a job here for a few months."

"Do they have children?"

Max drew out his wallet and flipped it

open to reveal a picture of a handsome, dark-haired man and a pretty blonde, blue-eyed woman and two towheaded youngsters. "That's Terry and Mitzie," he said.

"They must meet my son, Roycie," Autumn said in delight. "He's away with his grandmother but will be here soon."

"The children are still at home in Idaho until school is out, which shouldn't be long," Max said. "Their grandparents are with them."

"And what about you? Are you married?" Autumn asked.

"No," Max said. He hesitated, then asked, "Is your husband here with you?"

Autumn looked down at her slim hands for a moment, twisting the stunningly beautiful and expensive wedding ring back and forth for a moment before she said quietly, "My husband is dead."

"I'm sorry," Max said. He took a bite from the buttery roll, then asked, "Are the 'they' you were talking about nurses who take care of you?"

Autumn took a sip of coffee and set down the fragile china cup. Her laugh was soft and bell-like, "Yes — in a way. I suppose I'm making them sound like monsters, and they're not. They are really my older sister, Audra, Mother, and my younger brother,

Sherman. Also my physician, Dr. Marler, lives with us. He's semi-retired and a cousin of my mother's, so he just cares for our family now."

"You said you pass out often," Max said. "If you're that sick, shouldn't you be in the hospital?"

Autumn's eyes darkened and a spasm as of pain flickered over her lovely face. Then she looked directly into Max's face and said in an expressionless voice, "I'm terminally ill — bone cancer. Dr. Marler gives me no more than a few weeks at the most."

Max laid his roll on his plate and stared at Autumn. He felt as if she had thrown icy water in his face. For a moment he was too stunned to speak, then he blurted, "But-but are they sure? Couldn't there be a mistake?" His shocked mind recoiled from the possibility that this lovely creature was dying.

Autumn looked away from Max. Her eyes took on a strange, almost wistful expression. "There's no mistake. Another doctor confirmed the diagnosis. But it is probably for the best. I have been a curse to all those I love the best. It will almost be a relief to go where I can never hurt anyone again!"

2

Before Max could recover from this announcement, a door slammed and a tall, angular woman came striding across the lawn. Her auburn hair, streaked with grey, was drawn up into a loose french roll. Her stern face was set in angry lines.

Ignoring Autumn, she stopped before Max and spoke angrily, "How did you get in here? The servants have strict orders that *no* one is to invade our privacy!"

Hastily Max rose to his feet and spoke apologetically, "I'm the chauffeur from next door. I saw the lady lying on the steps, and I thought she was hurt."

"Well, she is all right now so I think you had better go back where you came from. Mrs. Caldwell is very ill and she doesn't need to be bothered."

"Audra," Autumn's soft voice was reproving, "this gentleman just came to help me, and he stayed at my invitation. He has only been here a few minutes and has not tired me in the least."

Audra's frown only deepened as she

glared at Max. "The doctor's express orders are that my sister have no visitors. She is not strong enough! Now go before I call your employers and have them order you home!"

"Audra!" A bright spot of color appeared in Autumn's pale cheeks, and she spoke sharply. "I'll not have you being rude to Max! Remember, this is my home. I'll not have you insulting my visitors!"

Obviously Audra was unaccustomed to Autumn standing up to her because she turned toward her sister with shock written plainly on her face. The asperity left her voice as she said in an injured tone, "Now Autumn, you know I am just trying to take care of you the best I know how, and those are the doctor's orders, not mine!"

"I know you are," Autumn said gently. "But . . ."

At the sharp tapping of a stick on the cobbled walk nearby, she broke off and turned her head toward the sound.

A small, fragile looking woman was approaching, clinging to the arm of a tall, skinny young man. Her other immaculately white-gloved hand held a black walking stick.

Without another word, Audra marched over to the newcomers, spoke briefly to the older woman, then walked away toward the house, her back stiff and disapproving.

The two walked to where Autumn and Max waited. "Max," Autumn said quickly, "this is my mother, Cecilia Cassel, and my brother, Sherman Cassel. Mother, Sherman, this is our neighbor, Max Parrish. We were having some refreshments. Would you like some?"

Cecilia's eyes were gentle but grave. "How do you do, Max? You are Mr. Windthorn's chauffeur, I believe."

Autumn's brother barely nodded when Max acknowledged the introduction. He busied himself with drawing up a chair for his mother. Then, seating himself slightly behind her, he stared insolently at Max.

Cecilia spoke gently to her daughter in a sweet, cultured voice, "You look very tired, dear. It isn't a good idea for you to have company. You aren't strong enough."

Without waiting for Autumn's answer, she turned fine grey eyes — so like Autumn's — to Max and spoke quietly but firmly, "I must ask you to leave us now. We must get Autumn to bed; I can see she has over-exerted herself. Thank you for coming, but I must insist that you not come again. As you can see, my dear daughter is not well."

"Sure," Max said. He turned toward

Autumn and saw that her finely-chiseled lips were trembling slightly.

"Mother," Autumn's soft voice shook slightly, "I-I have not overexerted myself! I may not have long to live but I would like to 'live' a little during that time. Being confined to my bed is not 'living'!"

Pain was mirrored in Cecilia's sweet face, "Autumn, dear we want to keep you as long as we can. If you don't let us take care of you, your days could be very short indeed."

Her voice quivered and broke, "This whole thing is so painful for me. Losing you while you are still so y-young is almost more than I can bear." Tears glistened on her long, dark lashes. "Please let us do what we think is best for you. We just want you with us as long as possible."

"I'm sorry, Mother. I didn't mean to make you cry," Autumn's voice had sunk to almost a whisper.

She rose, took an unsteady step toward Max, and said softly, "Thank you for coming. You-you made me feel almost w-well again. I will go in now. I am feeling a little faint." With a wan smile, she turned and walked slowly toward the house.

Audra hurried to meet her from the *corredore*, put her arm about her, and assisted her into the house.

"It was nice meeting you, young man," Mrs. Cassel said to Max with a smile. "It was good of you to come. I hope you understand our concern for my daughter. She is very ill. Good-bye now."

As Max said good-bye, she rose, took her son's arm and followed Autumn, tapping along the cobbled walk with her cane.

Max walked slowly back toward the still open dividing gate. His thoughts were in a turmoil. Autumn had seemed so alive while she talked with him — until her family appeared. They obviously loved her deeply but with a smothering love that was squeezing the remaining life out of the young woman.

If she is going to die anyway, what difference does it make if she does overtax herself some? he wondered. Wasn't quality of life more important than living a little longer?

He was so absorbed in his private thoughts that he started when his name was spoken sharply. Autumn's brother stood near him, directly under the arch of the large open gate.

"Yes?" Max asked.

Sherman Cassel's pale grey eyes were insolent in his slender, pimply face. "Max," the voice was high and thin, almost like a child's voice, "stay away from my sister.

19

That's an order!"

Max's gravelly voice was low but calm, "Whose order?"

"*My* order," Sherman's voice rose slightly. "Don't come back here again! Do you understand?"

Max felt his ire rising. Sherman's arrogant, condescending manner rasped keenly on his ego. But he kept a firm hand on his temper and said calmly, "I don't know that she will, but if Mrs. Caldwell does ask me to come, I see no reason to refuse.

"I agree with her; she should be able to enjoy herself as much as possible in the short time she has left to live. If I can help her feel better, then there's nothing wrong with that. It would be my pleasure!"

"Sure it would!" Sherman sneered. "As if I don't know what you're after! You know Autumn's rich, and you hope to weasel yourself into her affections! Well, it won't work, buster, so get lost and stay lost!"

Max's fists unconsciously balled into fists as anger lanced through him like a hot shaft. He breathed heavily for a moment, striving to master his temper before he answered.

Sherman's pale eyes narrowed warily as he backed slowly away.

Max's gaze locked with Sherman's like yellow fire, but his voice was calm when he spoke, "I've only just met your sister, and I know nothing about her or any of you. I only stayed for a few minutes to talk to her because she was lonesome and asked me to stay."

Sherman eased back a couple of more steps and then said scornfully, "Perhaps I should enlighten you a little about my dear sister. She killed her husband and spent a year in an institution for the insane because of it!"

Max felt like Sherman had hit him in the stomach. The impact showed plainly on his candid face.

Autumn's brother chuckled unpleasantly. "Shocking, isn't it?" He leaned forward, his face twisted with malicious glee. "And do you know something else, Max? Autumn Caldwell is a black widow!

"You know the peculiar habits of those darling female spiders, don't you? They kill the males when they are no longer useful to them? Well, all the men of my dear sister's life have died mysteriously, violently. That's why I keep my distance! And you would do well to do the same.

"Autumn Caldwell is as beautiful as a dream but watch out if she takes a liking to you! It isn't healthy!" With a chilling chuckle, Sherman turned and walked rap-

21

idly toward the house. He turned at the door, saluted mockingly, and disappeared inside.

Max walked slowly through the gate, absentmindedly shutting it behind him, into the Windthorn's patio. His mind reeled with shock. Surely the things Autumn's brother had said were not true!

He went to sit on the edge of the pool, a favorite spot. But the silvery spray from the mermaid's mouth and the lively jewel-like fish seemed to have dulled.

After a few moments, he rose with a sigh and ambled down the path to stand once more at the wrought-iron gate. The gate was locked again and the gardener was working on the other side, digging around some plants with a crude looking machete. There was no sound except for the dull scrape and jab of his blade.

A movement caught his attention, and Max lifted his eyes to the second floor of Autumn's hacienda. Autumn's pale face appeared briefly in a large window there and then he saw Audra lead her away.

Did Autumn really murder her husband? Max wondered. A year in a mental hospital . . . deranged people do horrible things sometimes. *Is it possible that Autumn is really insane? Mad?*

Max shook his head in disbelief. She certainly seemed sane to him. But he had heard that such people appeared fine at times. He was no doctor, so how could he tell who was mentally sound and who wasn't?

A sudden thought made him cringe as chills slid down his spine. What if that was why her family didn't allow her to have visitors? Maybe they were protecting others from the harm Autumn might do to them! Had her family persuaded the authorities to let Autumn come home to die in peace, surrounded by her caring family?

Max turned away from the gate and strolled along the cobbled path that circled the pool and then branched off to meander through the flowerbeds laid out in eye-pleasing designs of glorious color in flowers, rocks, shrubs, and trees. Usually he gloried in the beauty of the Mexican home the Windthorns had leased, but he didn't even notice it now as he paced restlessly. Sudden anger flared in Max's heart. It wasn't fair! That lovely woman — she could be no more than in her late twenties — condemned to such a painful death! It was heartbreaking!

Max swallowed hard, and walking quickly, he took a stone path that led into the wide *corredore* or gallery that encircled the large patio. Much of the family living was done here; it was open on one side and furnished with comfortable couches, chairs, and tables.

He walked across the tile floor and entered his own large, attractive quarters. Usually he paused at the door to savor the feeling of peace and delight the rooms brought to his spirit, long starved for beauty and comfort. But that peace was missing now.

He slowly climbed the spiral stairway that wound around the wide, circular chimney of his brick fireplace and stepped out onto the gallery above. He liked to pray up here; he could look down upon his small world and marvel at the goodness of God in giving him back his freedom and bringing him here. But the joy was gone today. Dispiritedly, he went back downstairs.

Kicking off his shoes, he lay down on his bed and stared morosely at the ceiling.

"Max," he said aloud, "why are you letting this dying girl get to you? You don't even know the woman! People die all the time. Who are you mad at? God?"

He considered. No. He wasn't angry with God. He wasn't mad at anyone in particular. Just angry with whatever caused a diabolical malignancy to attach itself to a beautiful woman like Autumn and slowly sap her life. And worse yet — if he could believe her brother — that this beautiful woman had been driven by madness to kill someone she loved! Not to mention the other dark deeds he had hinted at connected with the men of her life!

His spirit seemed to shrivel inside at the thought of the insidious, deadly destruction in the body and mind of this lovely young woman.

Suddenly he cried out, "Why, Father? Why?" Turning over on his stomach, he buried his face in his big hands and poured out his tormented thoughts. For a long while Max talked to the Lord. When he ceased, he still did not have the answers he sought, but his heart was at peace.

His thoughts rested again upon Autumn. If she was dying, it was important that he discover if she knew Jesus Christ. Even a mixed-up mind could reach out and find the Lord.

"I must find a way to talk with Autumn again," Max declared in the stillness of his room.

His heart seemed to do queer things at the thought of seeing her again, and Max told himself sternly, "You idiot! That gracious woman would never have noticed you existed if she had not been so desperate for company. Don't you forget it — or that she may be as deadly as a black widow!"

3

Skye Windthorn called that evening. "Joy and I are spending the night here, Max. But when we get home tomorrow night, we will be accompanied by four guests." Then Joy came on the line to give Max instructions for the dinner.

Max spent the evening alone, studying. When he had first become a Christian, in prison, he could barely read, but his desire to read the Bible had become a consuming thirst. He had eagerly attended the prison classes in English, reading, and writing. He was doggedly working his way through several college correspondence courses now, even one in beginning Spanish.

The next morning Max arose early, as was his custom. He prayed as he worked out in the well-equipped exercise room Skye had set up in a large room off the patio.

Then he came in and showered before giving his orders to Emilia, the pleasant, plump Mexican cook, for the dinner that evening. Telling her he would eat later, he went out into the patio, planning to sit at a stone table near the fountain to make a list of things he had to do that day.

As Max followed the stone path near the large wrought iron dividing gate, he heard his name called. His heart began to pound. It was Autumn's voice!

He tried not to show his eagerness to see her by walking — what he hoped appeared — casually over to the gate.

Autumn was reclining on a luxurious chaise lounge not far from the gate, under the shade of a tree. A pretty Mexican maid, uniformed in black and white, was laying a small round table for two, with a bright yellow cloth and brown dishes. Sitting on a serving table nearby was a silver coffee service and a yellow pottery platter laden with mangoes and bananas.

Rising gracefully, Autumn came over to the gate. With a warm smile, she extended her hand through the vertical bars to Max.

"Max, will you have breakfast with me? I hope you don't think I'm too forward, but I enjoyed our chat yesterday and wanted to talk some more, if you have the time."

Max felt his heart lurch with a feeling similar to pain. The woman was so bewitchingly beautiful! Dressed in a flowing robe of apple-green, her glowing russet red hair caught back with a matching scarf, she looked like a queen. Today, the only evidence of her illness was her willowy thinness.

The words of her brother suddenly dropped into his mind like shards of jagged ice: "Autumn Caldwell is as beautiful as a dream but watch out if she takes a liking to you! It isn't healthy!"

A chill traced its way down his back, but it vanished like vapor in the sun as he accepted her cool slim fingers into his hand. He heard himself assuring her that he was completely free for awhile.

Jorge came and opened the gate. In all of thirty-four years, Max had never felt like he did when Autumn laid her soft hand on his arm and led him to the table.

"Please sit down," Autumn waved to a comfortable cushioned chair at the table and slipped into one across from him. "I had Juana bring an assortment of things. Just help yourself to anything you like. Our cook has learned to make very good biscuits so I had her bake some — in case you have grown tired of the ever present tortillas we have here in Mexico."

A little quiver of alarm shot through Max. Why was this wealthy, attractive woman going to so much trouble for him?

Then Autumn smiled at him, banishing

the clouds of doubt. "Would you like coffee?"

"Yes, thank you," Max said. Autumn spoke to Juana in Spanish, and she poured out coffee for them both.

Max had expected to feel tongue-tied and ill-at-ease, but Autumn chatted easily, with a friendliness that was disarming and relaxing. Asking him about his life in Mexico and telling amusing little everyday incidents, she soon had him laughing and talking as if he had always known her.

He found himself talking freely and glowingly of his job with the Windthorns.

"The Windthorns are more than just my employers; they are wonderful friends. They visited me in prison, and then gave me a job when I got out."

"You were in prison?"

Steeling himself for the inevitable rejection, Max said, "I'm afraid so." Not allowing himself to analyze Autumn's reaction, he took out his billfold and showed her a picture of an attractive, dark-headed woman and blond man. "I was a jewel thief, but this couple became my friends and introduced me to Jesus Christ as my personal Savior. This is Carole and David Loring, some of the finest friends a guy ever had. They visited me regularly

30

while I was in prison, and encouraged me to take courses to help me when I got out.

"Because they are close friends of Joy and Skye Windthorn, it was through the Lorings that the Windthorns started visiting me. Then both families worked to get me out, and Mr. Windthorn gave me this job as his chauffeur and personal assistant. It means so much that they trust me," he finished softly.

Autumn was watching Max with wide-eyed absorption.

"I hope that doesn't make a difference to you," Max said earnestly, his eyes scanning hers intently, "that I am an ex-con, I mean. I used to be a jewel thief, but I've been out of prison a year. Believe me, since I found Jesus Christ, jewels don't mean a thing to me. The Lord Jesus Christ is the best jewel of them all.

"I used to hate everybody! And myself most of all. But that's all changed. There isn't anyone that I don't like now. And my greatest happiness is telling other people about Christ, who can make life worth living."

Max leaned toward Autumn and spoke with utmost seriousness, "Do you know Him, Autumn?" Max was so intent that he used her first name unconsciously.

A startled look came into Autumn's eyes, and she looked confused. "I-I don't know what you mean. I believe that Jesus came to earth and that He was God's Son."

"There's more to it than that, Autumn. Me, you, everybody has sinned. Jesus is God's Son, but He also died to pay for our sins. We must each one personally accept Jesus as God's gift of salvation to us. We ask him to forgive our sins and invite Him to take over our lives and help us to live for Him. And, let me tell you. He'll do just that! He just floods a person's life with His love."

Autumn stared at Max in astonishment. He was unaware that his rugged face and strange yellow eyes literally lit up as he talked about God. "You-you sound . . . like a preacher," she said.

Max grinned, suddenly self-conscious. "I hope to be someday — maybe a missionary. But right now I'm just working for a living and learning all I can."

Autumn spoke softly, "You frighten me a little. I never heard anyone talk about God like He is — so real. I-I'm not sure I like that. I've done so many things that I know He wouldn't approve of. . . ."

"So did I!" Max interrupted. "Devilish, awful things! But not any more. Christ took away my desire to do those things and gives me His strength to keep from falling back into those old ways.

"And," Max said with deep sincerity, "when a child of God leaves this life he — or she — will always be with Jesus. There will be no sickness or pain in that new home. . . ."

Autumn's eyes darkened suddenly as she interrupted, "I hate being sick. I wish you hadn't reminded me of that! Why does everyone keep reminding me that I'm going to die?"

"I'm sorry," Max said contritely, "I just thought. . . ."

But she wasn't listening to him. She turned her head toward the house and said morosely, "*They* treat me like an invalid so I can never forget for a moment that I'm dying."

"Except that you're thin, you certainly don't look that sick." Max grinned. "I don't know how you could look any more beautiful." Instantly, hot color flooded his face. He hadn't meant to say that; it had just popped out.

"Please don't say that!" Autumn's face had gone ashen. Anger glinted in her eyes. "I hate my beauty! It's been a curse to me all my life — and to everyone I ever loved!"

Max's throat went dry and tight. "B-but

that can't be true," he blurted out. "Just looking at you is like looking at a beautiful picture."

Autumn was shaking her head vehemently. "I wish I had been plain — then no one would ever have noticed me! My father loved me best because of my face! I knew it, and that Sherman resented it. When we were growing up, Audra treated me awful because of it. My school friends were jealous of me. I had no close friends, just those who attached themselves to me because I always attracted more boyfriends than I needed."

Tears were trembling on Autumn's thick lashes as she gazed at Max through misted, misery-laden eyes. Her voice sank to a whisper. "I wonder sometimes if my family only tolerates me because I made the fortune that supports them all in luxury. Not mother, of course, she loves us all equally and never plays favorites."

Autumn choked back a sob and lowered her head, "I know that is a terrible thing to say, but I have thought it for a long time. I've never dared to say it before, though."

Max didn't know what to say. He felt extremely uncomfortable, so just sat still and looked at her.

Autumn suddenly laughed self-consciously, and said humbly, "I expect you think I'm just feeling sorry for myself — and you're right, I am. Believe it or not, I don't often rant on this way. Of course my family loves me. They work hard at making me comfortable and are very concerned for me."

She drew in a long quivering breath, "I'm sorry to pour all my morbid thoughts out on you. You won't want to come again, and I wouldn't blame you. Forgive me, please?"

Her blue-grey eyes, still misty, looking into his so solemnly caused a catch in Max's throat.

He spoke quickly. "There's nothing to forgive. We all need to pour out our feelings now and then. And I'm a good listener anytime you need someone to talk to."

"Thank you, Max. You're so kind." With charming, childlike abruptness, happiness again glowed in her face. "It has been so good to have someone to talk to."

4

The dinner party that night went well, and the Windthorns were pleased. Skye excused Max after dinner, even though his guests would be staying the night.

"I know you like to study every night," Skye said. "Everything is under control, and the maid is here if we need anything. If we need you, I can always buzz you."

So Max retired gratefully to his quarters to study.

He brought his customary glass of Emilia's special concoction of juices that he liked so well and set it on his nightstand beside his Spanish lesson book and cassette player. Then he went to lock the two large gates, set in arches of stone, that protected the passageways leading into the large patio in the center of the house.

When he arrived back in his room, he dressed for bed — laying out his bathrobe to use for his final check of the grounds, gates, and doors before he went to sleep later that night — and climbed into bed with a sigh.

He finished his juice within a few minutes

as he listened to his Spanish lesson on tape, following along in the lesson book and repeating the sentences during the pause after each line.

He was pleased with his growing proficiency in the Spanish language. To the vast amusement of the cook, maids, and Jorge, he tried out his new words and phrases on them continually, as well as in the markets and stores. Emilia, the cook, teased him about his mistakes, but he knew she was pleased that he wished to learn Spanish and helped him immensely by correcting his accent and pronunciation.

About an hour later, he felt himself grow very sleepy and even slightly faint. He considered turning off the cassette player and going to sleep, but decided to finish the lesson first.

Suddenly, pale violet shadows floated over the lesson page. A little alarmed, he closed his eyes, but the violet shadows were still there, only more intense, drifting about under his closed eyelids.

He opened his eyes and shook his head sharply. He looked about the room and each object seemed edged in purest black with a background of changing, drifting colors.

A strange lethargy was spreading slowly through his body, but it seemed he had neither the power nor the desire to fight it. A euphoric feeling of well-being was slowly washing away any desire to do anything but lay back and let this feeling wash over and through him.

Bright colors and indistinct, but fascinating, shapes drifted about the room, growing brighter and more intense.

Suddenly there seemed to rise out of the floor a figure — a strange creature with arms and legs that writhed and wove. He didn't know if the figure was real or fantasy — nor did he care.

The figure danced about the room, weaving in and out of the floating, shifting clouds of brilliant colors and forms. Suddenly it dipped and moved closer and closer to Max until its leering, dark face with coarse, white beard and hair, was very near his face. Its hand swept around and passed before his eyes. In the gloved hand was an apple green scarf, fantastically lovely to his enraptured senses.

He closed his eyes for a moment, and when he opened them the figure was no longer there among the kaleidoscope of shimmering, swirling colors. He felt no surprise — or fear.

The euphoric feeling slid over him like a warm, delicious bath, and he gave himself up to the ever changing, ever deepening colors and shapes. The last thing Max remembered were the reds, oranges, purples, and yellows, brilliant beyond description, and the whites, shimmering and pure, the blacks, glistening and breathtaking.

Morning arrived with the clamoring of Max's alarm clock. Usually he was awake when it went off, but not today. He reached over and turned off its jarring sound and lay back, feeling tired and strangely lethargic. Then he remembered! The dream!

It was still vivid in his mind. He had never had such a dream in his life! It was almost too real to be a dream but, of course, it had to be. He closed his eyes and could almost see again the vivid colors and odd, ever changing shapes. He struggled to recall other details of the strange dream.

Hadn't there been a figure, wearing a Mexican mask, swaying and dancing among the shifting, changing lights and shapes? It had come very near him, in the dream, and danced about him with a scarf in its hand.

Max sat up on the side of the bed reluctantly. He wanted to think some more about his vivid dream, but he had work to do. He had apparently fallen asleep so deeply that he had not even made his final check of the premises last night. Could he have been that tired?

Shaking his head in disgust at himself, because he prided himself on caring for his employers and their possessions with extra diligence, Max slipped off the side of the bed and padded over to his chest of drawers.

His bare foot trod on something soft and silky. He stooped and picked it up. Then his heart seemed to leap into his throat and pound there like a drum. In his hand was an apple-green scarf — the one Autumn had been wearing at breakfast the morning before.

He backed up and sat down heavily. His mind was reeling with shock. Surely he was mistaken! He raised the scarf and looked at it again. The faint odor of perfume titillated his nostrils — Autumn's perfume!

A cold hand seemed to clutch at his middle. The dream last night was no dream!

Sudden fear beat in his throat, and his mouth felt as dry as desert sand. Was he losing his mind? What had happened to him last night? Max didn't have much fear of man, but this was something different. Something uncanny and weird.

"Father, please help me to think this thing out calmly." His words sounded strange and far away to his own ears. But as he repeated the request, he felt the turmoil in his chest begin to subside. He took two deep gulps of air and let out his breath slowly. He began to replay in his mind what had transpired last night, step by step.

He recalled getting dressed for bed, getting his regular glass of cold juice, and locking the gates. Sipping his juice, he had listened to his nightly Spanish lesson on cassette tape and repeated each line while following along in his lesson book. Very ordinary things that he did every night.

When had he first noticed the beginning of the strange lights? He considered. Not for quite a while because he could still remember Spanish words he had learned last night. Even several complete lines of Spanish from his lesson book reeled off in his mind from the cassette.

Ah! He had turned off the cassette player when the violet shadows began to play across his book. He grabbed the lesson book and found where he had shut off the recorder. He had almost finished a lesson. Quickly he calculated about how long he had worked on the lesson. Probably more than an hour.

Emilia's special concoction of fruit juices. It was the only explanation. He usually drank a whole glass in a few minutes. Had there been something in his drink last night?

He pondered. The vivid visions, the sense of euphoric well-being, the uncertainty of what was reality and what was fantasy — it all smacked of some kind of drug, something that would cause hallucinations or visions.

Cold fear crawled up Max's neck and sweat broke out on his forehead. He had a morbid terror of using drugs of any kind. His mother would have sold her soul for another fix. Drugs had been her god and master. He had done many things in his wayward life — horrible things that made him cringe at their memory even now — but he had never tried drugs but once.

He had stolen some marijuana from his mother and smoked it.

He still recalled the feeling it had generated and the beating his mother had given him when he came out of his dream-like state. That was before she had gone off the deep end into drugs. As she beat him, she had screamed at him about all the horrors of becoming hooked on drugs. She didn't want a junkie for a son, she had screamed, accenting each word with a vicious lash of a man's belt.

Her treatment — both words and lashes — made such an impression on Max, coupled with her own horrible example a little later, that he had never again sampled or used drugs.

Max shook his head in unbelief. He had been given an hallucinogenic drug last night. He was sure of it. And almost without a doubt by Autumn. Why?

It would have been a simple matter while I was checking the locks on the gates last night, he reasoned. *And Autumn does seem to be a very mixed-up, hurting person right now.*

He looked down at the scarf still in his hand. The silkiness felt good in his fingers. Abruptly he threw it down on the floor as if it were a snake. The words of Autumn's brother, Sherman, had suddenly dropped into his mind like searing coals of fire: "Autumn Caldwell is a black widow! Watch out if she takes a liking to you! It isn't healthy!"

Sweat broke out all over Max's body and yet he felt like he was going to have a chill. Could Sherman be telling the truth? Did Autumn have some strange, warped obsession that drove her to draw men to her so she could kill them?

But if she had wanted to kill him, couldn't she have killed him just as easily as drugging him? A shiver crawled along his backbone. Maybe she wasn't ready to kill him yet. Perhaps she was playing out some strange fantasy — playing with him — while drawing him deeper and deeper into her web.

Maybe she was addicted to drugs herself. Knowing she was dying anyway and in pain frequently, the doctor who lived with them and cared for her would logically give her all she wanted.

Through his mother, Max had known many drug addicts. He knew some of the weird, unnatural things some did under the influence of drugs. His mother's only real friend had hacked her baby to pieces while under the influence of LSD. Later that night, she had robbed a drugstore with the same butcher knife and swallowed enough drugs of different kinds to kill several people.

After her friend's death, Max remembered how his mother had gone berserk, screaming and cursing and tearing her hair. He had gone out and stolen some drugs for her because he couldn't stand her insane screaming. He was only eleven at the time.

He shuddered now in remembrance. As abusive and uncaring as she had been to him and his sister, Tina, she had still been his mother. It was painful to know that she had died without God or hope! Dead of an overdose of heroin, when he was only fourteen years old.

His thoughts jumped back to Autumn. How had she gotten in? He went to his door. It opened easily in his hand. He had not locked it. Feeling secure with all the outside doors and gates locked, Max rarely bothered to lock the doors to his quarters.

It would have been so easy for Autumn to have a key made to the dividing gates. She could have spied on him, learned his nightly routine, slipped into his room while he was locking the gates, and drugged his juice. Obviously, she had hidden somewhere and come out after he was thoroughly under the influence of the drug. The thought was chilling.

But why would she want to drug him? There seemed to be no reason for her to do so. That was what frightened him.

And what had she used to drug him? There was little doubt the drug had been put in his juice.

Suddenly he leaped to his feet. The glass! If the drug had been put in his juice glass, there would be a residue of the drug still there, a residue that could be analyzed by a chemist for content. Also, there might be fingerprints on the glass.

Where had he put the glass? The bedside table, of course. His eyes darted over the few items there. The glass was not one of them. He searched the room, then his bathroom and sitting room.

His juice glass was gone.

5

A short while later, Max left his room and went in search of his employer. Skye was also an early riser, and he and Max quite often worked out together in the private gym Skye had set up.

When Max entered the gym, Skye looked up from the weights he was lifting and grinned. "You must have had a late night of study. I beat you over here this morning."

"I had a weird night," Max said gravely. "Do you have time to talk? Private like."

"Sure," Skye said quickly. "My guests and Joy are still in bed, so we shouldn't be disturbed. How about a cup of coffee? There's a pot plugged in over there and some of Emilia's nut-rolls."

Over coffee and rolls, Max told Skye about his experience of the night before.

Skye listened intently, without a word, until Max had finished. As Max talked, a frown furrowed Skye's forehead and his dark eyes narrowed. When he spoke his lean face was solemn, "This is serious. Do you have any idea who drugged you?"

Max hesitated, "It's hard to believe, but it sure looks like Autumn Caldwell, the lady next door."

"I didn't know you even knew the people next door," Skye said in astonishment. "Whatever makes you think someone from there drugged you?"

"I know it sounds crazy," Max said, "but I don't see how it could be anyone else."

He told Skye briefly about his meeting with Autumn and her family, about Sherman's warning, and that he had breakfasted with Autumn. "Autumn — Mrs. Caldwell — says she is dying of cancer."

"Yes, Victorio Sanchez, the landlord, told us that," Skye said. "He said they wanted absolutely no visitors." Skye's eyes twinkled. "You didn't mention that she is a very beautiful woman. Victorio seemed quite impressed with her."

Max felt his face grow hot for some inexplicable reason, but said earnestly, "She's the most beautiful woman I've ever met. She carries herself like a queen but doesn't act high and mighty. That's why I can hardly imagine her drugging me. The only reason she invited me to breakfast was because she was lonesome," he said quickly.

"What makes you think she, not someone else, entered your room and drugged you?"

"The odd figure who danced about in my room was waving a green scarf. When I woke up this morning, this was lying in my room." Max pulled Autumn's soft, silk scarf from his pants pocket and handed it to Skye. "Mrs. Caldwell was wearing this green scarf yesterday when we had breakfast together."

Skye took the strip of filmy silk and turned it to scan the tiny label in the hem, "This came from an exclusive women's shop in the States," Skye said. "I'll admit this scarf is damaging evidence, but it doesn't prove Mrs. Caldwell drugged you or was even in your room. Almost anyone could have had access to this. Someone could be trying to make you think she did it so you'll stay away from her."

Raw, undisguised hope flared in Max's somber eyes. He said eagerly, "Do you think so? Maybe Sherman did it. Autumn — Mrs. Caldwell — seems like such a sweet, honest person. It's hard to believe she would drug a person — or kill her husband like her brother said."

Skye's forehead knotted in perplexity. "Autumn Caldwell — where *have* I heard that name before?" For a moment he was silent, then he burst out, "Of course! Autumn Caldwell, the stage star! For several years she was the rage. A little over two years ago she dropped out of sight, and no one seemed to know what became of her."

"A stage star!" Max exclaimed. "She looks like one, but she's so nice, it doesn't seem possible."

"I saw her on the stage twice. You're right, she does have 'class.' She's a marvelous actress and a talented singer, as well. I understand her husband directed her career and amassed a fortune for her. Her brother said she killed her husband? I never heard that."

"Could we check out Sherman's story?" Max asked.

"We could sure try. I'll be glad to do the checking if you want me to." Skye paused and then went on, "But you may not like what we find out. She could be just what Sherman says she is — a psychopathic killer."

"I know," Max said gravely.

"All right. I'll get right on it," Skye said. He laid his hand on Max's shoulder. "Max, in the meantime, please be careful. The girl seems to like you. If there *is* truth in Sherman Cassel's accusations, you might be in real danger."

For two days, Max did not hear or see anything of Autumn. One part of him was relieved, but another, inexplicable side of him longed for just a glimpse of her. Still, he dreaded meeting her again with the dark suspicions tumbling about in his brain. If only they were wrong!

He stayed busy, but whenever he was in the patio — and he found himself there often — his eyes seemed to travel of their own volition to the gate which separated the two places. But the patio remained empty except for Jorge working in the two yards.

In answer to his inquiries about Autumn, Jorge confided that a maid who worked there said the lady was very sick and confined to her room. Max wondered if Autumn was avoiding him. Or had she gotten high on some drug and was sick from it? She might have drugged him and not even known she did. His heart plummeted at such a thought — but he knew he had to consider every possibility — however painful.

The third day Skye called Max into his study. When he saw Skye's solemn face, Max knew the news was not good.

Motioning Max to a chair, Skye spoke quietly, "Max, I'm afraid at least part of Cassel's information is a matter of public record. Autumn Caldwell was convicted of killing her husband, Royce Caldwell, about two years ago and was sent to a mental institution. She was there for over a year. Her family was somehow able to obtain her release, and she has been in seclusion here in Mexico City ever since."

Max felt like he had been doused in ice water. "A-are you sure there's no mistake?"

"I'm sure," Skye said. "I'm very sorry, Max. I really am!"

"T-thanks for checking out Sherman's story," Max muttered. He felt a numbing sensation in his brain, and he felt slightly nauseous. He had not realized how much he had been hoping Sherman's story was not true.

He rose to leave the room, and then a sudden thought came to him. "How did she do it?"

"Poison. Autumn always fixed her husband a nightly cup of coffee, sugar, chocolate, and cream. He felt it helped him to sleep, and it was sort of a ritual with them. She always prepared it herself and brought it to him after he was in bed.

"Her family lived with them, even as they do now. The record says that on that particular night, her family recalled that she seemed highly agitated and not quite herself."

"Did anyone see Autumn make the drink?" Max asked through tight lips.

"I'm afraid so, Max. The cook testified that she was in the kitchen when Mrs. Caldwell came in, made her husband's drink and carried it away. She also verified the family's testimony that Mrs. Caldwell seemed 'strung-out' and nervous."

"Strung-out?" Max asked. "Was she on drugs?"

"Well, I don't know that she was a drug addict, but her doctor prescribed drugs for her, some to keep her going and some to make her sleep. She was under a heavy load at that time with her acting."

"I suppose someone saw her take the drink in to her husband?"

"Her sister saw her go in the room with the cup in her hand. A few minutes after she took the drink to Royce, Autumn's screams were heard. The cook, a maid, and Autumn's mother, brother and sister all rushed to the room. Royce was dead, lying in their bed with the empty cup nearby. Autumn was in hysterics and was babbling that she had killed her husband."

"So she admitted killing her husband?" Max said. His chest felt like an elephant was sitting on it, but he felt he must know everything.

"Yes, there never seemed to be any doubt that she did. Her mother's cousin is a doctor. Due to ill health, he was semi-retired and had made his home with them for quite a while. He was summoned from his room and declared Royce dead. Then he administered a strong sedative to Autumn because she went completely to pieces."

"How long was she that way?" Max asked. "I mean, she was mentally unbalanced for awhile after that?"

"That, I don't know. And also, I haven't heard yet if Sherman's other claims are true — that other men she was connected with emotionally died under strange circumstances. I've got some inquiries out. We should know more very soon."

"Thanks, boss. I'd better get back to work." Max moved to the door, dejection stamped clearly on his face.

"Max," Skye followed him to the door, "I can see you like Autumn. Don't let this news get you down. Remember, we can't live other people's lives for them. And what's done cannot be changed." He laid his hand on Max's arm. "I *would* feel better if you steered clear of that woman."

Max stood for a moment without speaking, staring at the floor. Then he lifted pain-filled eyes to his employer's face. "I've never cared much for women, maybe because my mother was such a disappointment to me. But Autumn has gotten to me. She seems so — so defenseless, so fragile and — and lonely."

Max shook his big head in bewilderment. "I can't figure out why she affects me this way. It's something about the way she carries herself — like a queen — and yet she makes me feel good about myself."

Max seemed to forget Skye as his oddly-colored yellow eyes glowed and his husky voice softened, "And she is so beautiful that she nearly takes my breath away. When I'm around her, I feel like I'd like to protect her and shield her from hurtful things."

Suddenly Max's face flamed red and he ducked his head, "I know it's crazy, but I can't help the way I feel . . . even though I know she killed her husband, and probably sneaked into my room and drugged me."

"It could be dangerous," Skye said gently, "in many ways. If Autumn is a psychopath, your life could be in real danger if you continue to see her. Even if she is not, she apparently has serious mental problems."

Max started to speak but Skye continued determinedly, "Another very real danger is you could end up with a broken heart. That can be a very painful experience. I know! Such an experience nearly wrecked my life, before I met Joy. And, from what you've told me, Autumn's not a Christian.'"

"Now wait a minute, boss," Max said. "With this ugly mug of mine, I'm not dumb enough to think that a gorgeous lady like Autumn would ever consider me as anything but a friend. Besides, she only has a short time to live and a sweetheart would be the farthest thing from her mind. I know she is just desperate for someone to talk to besides her family. She told me so."

Max's face took on a resolute look. "I don't see why it would hurt to talk to her whenever I can. Maybe I can be a help to her." A look that bordered on defiance came into his eyes and his jaw firmed stubbornly. "Even if she is a murderer, she needs a friend."

"True — true," Skye hastened to say, "but I just don't want to see you get hurt in some way — or worse. That's my only concern. Part of Sherman's story has proven to be true so the rest could be, too.

"And don't forget, if she did drug you, she was cunning enough to get into your room and out again without being discovered. Be sure and lock your doors securely. Don't take any chances.

"I can't tell you not to see her, but do be careful — if you decide to see her again. Be very careful!"

6

After dinner that evening, the Windthorns and their guests went out to a concert. Soon afterward, Max retired to his room to study.

As usual, he first opened his literature book, but he couldn't seem to keep his mind on the lesson. His conversation with Skye kept intruding.

In disgust, he slammed the book closed and tried to study a math lesson. But in the middle of a problem, he suddenly realized his mind had drifted off and he was thinking of Autumn. Was she really a murderer? Was she insane? His mind recoiled from both possibilities.

Skye had said there had never been any doubt that Autumn had killed her husband. But it was difficult for him to reconcile himself to that fact. How could that charming woman commit murder? And why? What had driven her to such lengths?

What if she really was a psychopathic killer? A chill whispered along his nerves. A cold-blooded, compulsive killer?

Restlessly, Max tossed aside his book and

rose to pace the floor.

He summoned Autumn's face to his memory — an easy task. Her clear, frank grey-blue eyes, her gentle, bell-like voice, and warm smile belied every evidence that she could kill anyone.

But could a person trust a face — a smile? The girl was an actress and a good one. Perhaps she had a delicate temperament and could not stand up under the rigors of her heavy schedule. Could Autumn's nerves have snapped so that she could not help what she had done?

Suddenly, Max felt as if the walls of the room were pressing in upon him. He snatched up two books and quickly went out his door onto the *corredore* which encircled the patio-garden. He and the Windthorns spent a lot of time here. Roofed and tile-floored, with one side open to the patio, it had the benefits of both indoors and outdoors.

Laying the books on a small round table, Max sank down in a comfortable cushioned rocker and sighed. A single lamp glowed in his part of the gallery but two large lamps lit up the patio, turning the fountain into a rainbow of sparkling droplets. The sound of traffic reached him faintly. Scents of jasmine and other heady blossom odors tantalized his nostrils and he smiled.

This was the time of day he most enjoyed: when the day's work was over and he could talk with God alone. The peacefulness of the garden seeped into his spirit, soothing away the restlessness.

Laying his tawny head on the back of the chair, Max began to pray. As usual, a deep thankfulness welled up inside him, a thankfulness so great that he felt his chest would burst. A joy surged through him so sweet that it brought tears to his eyes. He no longer had to run from the law! He was no longer a slave to savage anger and bitterness that could only be assuaged through hurting and abusing people. How blessed he was to be at peace with God, himself, and all men! What a joy to know — really know — Jesus Christ!

With his eyes closed, Max was so lost in prayer that he didn't know he wasn't alone until a soft voice spoke his name. Slowly he lifted his head and opened his eyes.

Autumn stood a few feet away, silhouetted against the sparkling spray of the fountain.

He came quickly to his feet, his heart pounding. But this time not from the nearness of the beautiful woman. Something was wrong — very wrong.

Autumn's lovely face was as pale as wax, she looked drawn and haggard; her eyes were wide, glassy looking, and appeared too large for her slim face.

"What is it?" Max asked as he moved swiftly across the patio to her.

Autumn made two starts to form words before any sound came out, then only a thread of a whisper, "Max, I-I'm afraid."

Max reached out and took her slim hands in his large ones. They were icy. "What are you afraid of, Autumn?" he asked anxiously.

When she continued to stare at him with wide frightened eyes, Max tightened his hold on her hands, "Tell me, Autumn, what's wrong?"

"I-I. . . ." Autumn suddenly crumpled. Max caught her before she fell, lifted her in his arms, and carried her to a lounge on the *corredore*. Again he marveled at how light she was for her height.

She lay with her eyes closed for several minutes, her breath coming in short, spasmodic bursts. Twice she grimaced and curled into a ball, her hands clenched against her abdomen as if she were in agony.

Max stood as if petrified. Autumn was very sick, but he was unsure what to do. He should go for help, but he was afraid to leave her alone. If only the servants were here! But the cook had already gone home and the live-in maid was out on a date. Suddenly, he remembered there was a doctor next door, Autumn's cousin.

"Autumn, I'm going to leave you for a minute," he said urgently. "I'll get the doctor who lives at your house."

Autumn's eyes flew open and she gasped, "No, please don't! I-I'll be all right soon. I always am." Closing her eyes again, she began to draw in deep droughts of air. A minute later another spasm of pain once again gripped her, but seemingly not as severe and for a briefer time. Once more she breathed in deeply a few times, then opened her eyes and smiled tremulously.

"See," she whispered, "I'm getting better now."

"Would some water help?" Max asked.

"Yes-yes, please," she said faintly.

Max dashed away and quickly returned with a glass of cold water. Lifting her head, he held the glass to her pale lips and she drank thirstily.

Lying back as if exhausted, Autumn spoke softly, "Thank you, Max. Could you get me a pillow? I think I can sit up in a minute."

Max placed a pillow under her head and shoulders. He was still alarmed at the lack of color in her face, but she did seem to be getting stronger. Perhaps a little color was coming back into her face, too. Her eyes were open now and a slight smile curved her lips.

She shifted her body and tried to sit up, but Max protested and urged her to lie still until she was stronger.

"I am much better, really I am," Autumn said. Her voice was, indeed, stronger and the spasms seemed to have passed.

After a moment, she drew herself up higher on the pillow, and Max hastened to bring another large pillow for her back.

"I'm very sorry to be so much trouble," Autumn said. Her grey eyes appeared smoky green in the subdued light.

Although it wasn't that warm, her dark red hair clung damply about her face where it straggled free from a restraining yellow silk scarf that held her hair back from her face. A full, loose, yellow Mexican dress — embroidered with large birds in brilliant blue, scarlet and green plumage — covered Autumn's thin body.

"No trouble," Max assured her. "Now, tell me what happened."

For a full moment she searched his face, then spoke earnestly, "I took my medicine as usual tonight. It always makes me a little ill, but tonight I felt terrible almost immediately. It was a feeling I can't describe. I wondered if I was going to die."

She lowered her eyes and spoke softly, "I thought I was prepared to die but I'm not! I was terrified! You seemed so kind, and my folks are —" she hesitated, "oh, I don't know. They are good to me, but we are not a-a demonstrative family."

She lifted solemn eyes to Max's face. "I have been too weak and sick to leave my room the past two days and have thought a lot about what you said the other day — about God. And then a while ago — when I took my medicine — I was sicker than I have ever been."

Tears rose in her lovely eyes. "If I was going to d-die, I wanted someone with me who is on speaking terms with H-Him. I-I even tried to talk to Him but — it didn't seem to work."

"How did you get the gate open?" Max asked.

Autumn lowered her eyes; long thick lashes swept down and shielded them from his gaze. "I bribed Jorge to have a key made for me after you came over for breakfast the other day. My family wouldn't like it, but if I ever needed help, I knew you could be counted on."

Suddenly a slight chill snaked through Max. Sherman Cassel's words sprang to mind. "Autumn Caldwell is as beautiful as a dream, but watch out if she takes a liking to you! . . . All the men of my dear sister's life have died mysteriously, violently."

Max tried to push the warning away, but it returned like a persistent mosquito. Was Autumn really dangerous? Was she a multiple killer? Even Skye had been uneasy about her.

Max suddenly realized that Autumn's eyes were on his face, puzzled and questioning. "What's wrong, Max?" she said softly. "You have a very expressive face. . . ."

She broke off and laughed suddenly, a bitter, brittle sound that rasped on his ears. "You've heard something! Probably from my brother! I'm right, aren't I? Sherman has gotten to you. . . ."

Max felt the hot blood rushing to his face, but he didn't take his eyes from Autumn's face, "Was Sherman telling the truth?" he asked gently.

Fiery-red spots appeared on Autumn's high cheekbones and sparks flashed in her eyes, "Did I kill my husband? Yes, I did! Are you satisfied?"

She tried to rise but a sudden spasm of pain crossed her face, and she fell back

64

gasping, pressing her stomach hard with her crossed arms.

Max quickly stood up and leaned over her, "Are you all right? Don't you think I should get you some help? The doctor, maybe?"

"No-no! Please don't!" After a moment, Autumn drew in a deep breath and slowly sat up. "I-I'm all right now." Her voice sounded weary and flat. She rose to her feet, holding to the edge of the lounge.

Steadying herself with a hand on a table, she spoke in an emotionless voice, "I'll be going now." Slowly she began walking across the tile floor of the *corredore*.

Max watched her slow progress until she stepped out into the patio. His thoughts were in a turmoil. His heart swelled with empathy as he watched her go. She seemed so fragile and — and so alone. How well he knew the pain of being alone — friendless in a world of people.

He moved swiftly and caught her arm before she took a second step into the yard, "Autumn, please come back. I think you need someone to talk to, and I meant it when I said I'm a good listener."

Autumn stopped and looked up at him with sad eyes, eyes that were suddenly swimming in tears. She turned her head away and dabbed at them with a balled fist, her voice was tremulous and muffled.

"You don't understand, Max. I really did kill my husband. I'm a murderer. There's nothing else to say. The court convicted me and — and sent me away to that horrible, frightening p-place."

A sob shook her thin form and she put her hands over her eyes. Max took her arm firmly and led her to a large upholstered chair. For several moments, Autumn sobbed, her head bent and her body shaking. Max, sitting beside her, pressed a large white handkerchief into her hands and after a time she wiped her eyes and blew her nose.

Looking up at him through still misty eyes, she laughed self-consciously. "I-I'm sorry. I-I seem to be always saying that to you."

She's even beautiful when she's crying, Max thought incredulously. Most people have red, swollen eyes but not Autumn Caldwell.

"Would you like some coffee or something cold?" Max asked.

"Something cold would be lovely," Autumn said gratefully.

Max went to the kitchen and returned soon with a pitcher, two glasses, two small plates, napkins, and a plate of assorted crackers and sweet rolls. Setting the tray on a small table, he drew it close to Autumn's chair and moved a chair for himself close by. He poured a glass of fruit juice for Autumn and set a plate for her.

Pushing the plate of crackers and sweet rolls toward her he said, "Help yourself. The juice is a mixture that our cook fixes. It's very good."

Taking a sip, Autumn said, "It is delicious." For a moment her thick, dark eyelashes swept down to her pale ivory cheeks, then she raised tragic eyes to Max's face. "You are wondering how I could kill my husband, I imagine."

"Does it bother you to talk about your husband?" Max asked.

"Yes, but maybe it would help to talk about it," Autumn said. Taking a deep breath, she said, "I met Royce Caldwell when I first began to try to break into the theater. He was a director, and as soon as he saw me do a tiny part in a play, he sought me out and said I had real potential.

"I allowed him to take over my life and in an amazingly short time he had molded me into a star. I blindly followed all of his suggestions and orders. He was a marvel as a director and manager, and I owe my success as a stage star to his directing and managing of my career."

She paused and Max asked, "So gratitude grew into love for your director and manager?"

Autumn considered. "Love? I don't think you love someone like Royce Caldwell. I idolized him and obeyed him. But I never got close to him as a man." She paused and looked away into space, seeming to struggle for words. "I think I was like a piece of living clay to him, something to be owned and molded and perfected."

"What was he like?"

"He was a perfect gentleman, although impatient at times. Cold, cultured, highly intelligent and disciplined. Royce not only managed my career, he invested my money as well — and extremely wisely. I am a very rich woman, and I have never handled a penny of my money.

"He even set up my income in such a way that no one, not even myself, or my family, could get our hands on all of it and foolishly squander it. That way I will always have a good income. He said I knew nothing of business and it was necessary. It is tied up like that for as long as I live."

"He was quite a man," Max said admiringly. He looked down at his big hands for a moment and then looked straight at

Autumn and spoke gently, "Why did you kill your husband?"

Autumn met his gaze with direct, troubled eyes, "I don't know."

7

"You mean you had no motive for wanting your husband dead?" Max asked incredulously.

Autumn looked down at her hands, clasped tightly in her lap. "The psychiatrists at the mental hospital believe I felt manipulated and — and used by Royce. When he would book me up with more than I felt I could perform, I often raged at him that he was killing me."

She looked up at Max. "But my anger never perturbed Royce. He was always calm, even a little amused, I think, with my anger." Her eyes took on a strange expression and she looked away. "He knew that in the end I would give in to him. I always did."

Quick resentment flashed into her eyes. "I have spent my life being dominated by those around me! My father — whom I loved dearly — also dominated me. Both he and my mother had been actors but not very successful ones. So he was determined that I would become the great and famous star of the family. He began my training before I can even remember. I had no choice in the matter!"

"Is he still living?" Max saw Autumn had drained her glass of juice so he refilled it and handed it to her.

Autumn accepted the glass and took a long drink. "This is very good," she said. "I think I will try one of those rolls, too. I'm suddenly famished." She selected one, broke it in two pieces and bit into one. "Ummm, this seems to hit the spot." She looked up. "Now what were you saying?"

"Is your father still alive?" Max asked again.

There was a sudden silence, then Autumn said, "No. He died a long time ago."

Max sensed a withdrawing in her, but he prodded gently anyway. "What happened to him?"

For a long moment Autumn sat silent, the roll in her hand seemingly forgotten. Max wondered if she was going to answer. Finally without looking at him, she said in a voice so low that he could scarcely hear her, "He jumped from a four-story window. From *my* bedroom window."

A chill like an arctic wind swept through Max. Sherman had spoken the truth! His throat seemed to close up until he could scarcely breathe. Was this beautiful woman a destroyer — of those she cared for the most?

Autumn laid the roll on her plate and raised her eyes to Max. Intense pain shone in their vivid depths. "Max, death seems to stalk those I care about the most. W-what is wrong with me? Am I possessed by a-a demon — or something?"

"Of course you aren't possessed by a devil!" Max defended her without even considering. "I'm sure you were in no way to blame!"

Autumn's face twisted with pain, and her whisper was a thread of anguish, "But those aren't the only ones!" Her voice rushed on as if she wanted to put it all out in the open for him to see.

"When I was a senior in high school, I was going with the football captain — a big, handsome guy. We were crazy about each other."

Her voice broke, but she gulped and rushed on, "We were out in a small boat, just he and I. A larger boat flashed by and caused a huge wave to slam against our boat. It overturned. B-Bob was an excellent swimmer, but t-the boat must have hit his h-head. I couldn't even try to help him because I could scarcely swim enough to keep afloat. I managed to grab the side of the boat and cling there until help came, but Bob never came up at a-all."

Horror crushed in upon Max, and he knew what the telling of this must be costing Autumn. "You don't have to tell me these things," he said gently through taut lips. "I know it must hurt deeply — just the remembering."

But Autumn did not seem to hear him. Her face in the subdued light was like pale marble, deathlike.

"And Bob was only the first. A few weeks after Royce died, my doctor committed suicide. Luther Reisner was Royce's doctor, and he became mine shortly after Royce began to manage my career. I always ran to him when life became more than I c-could t-take. He gave me tranquilizers and other pills to help me through whatever emergency I was in, while being careful I didn't become addicted.

"But Luther also cared about me — personally. After Royce died, he confided that he had loved me from the first time he saw me, and he wanted to marry me when a proper time had passed. He was a fine man."

She turned tortured eyes to Max's face. "He committed suicide by jumping from my bedroom window — just as my father had done several years before. And both men had so much to live for! They were vibrantly alive, not depressed or in any kind of trouble — or anything. Why, Max? Why did they take their own lives? And — and from my room!"

Max was silent. His eyes held sympathy but no words would come. What could he say? He did not know the answers and dismay had stupefied his brain. Was there such a thing as a curse? Or had this lovely girl somehow managed to murder the other men, too? It seemed too preposterous for serious consideration, but the facts were there, spoken from Autumn's own lips: four men — all close to Autumn — had died.

Autumn's voice took on a bitter edge. "The newspapers had a heyday with all of this when Royce and then Dr. Reisner died. They even dredged up the old stories about Bob and my dad and — and splashed them across the front pages of the newspapers.

"When Luther died, he had come to visit me at home. He had managed to get me out of the mental hospital where I was being held. I'm not sure exactly how except I know he assured them that a nurse/guard would be with me at all times, and I would be confined to my own room."

Max found his voice. "Where were you when your father and the doctor jumped from your bedroom window?"

"I have thought so many times that perhaps I could have kept them from doing it if I had been aware of what was happening. When my father died, it was in the early hours of the morning. I had taken a sleeping pill and when the sounds of police sirens woke me, my father was already dead. The yard was full of shocked people, police cars, and an ambulance."

"Did anyone actually see your father leap to his death?"

"Yes, my sister, Audra, did. She said she had awakened for some reason, looked out her window, and saw there was a light in my room. Then . . . then Father leaped to his death in front of her eyes."

"What about the doctor? Do you remember any of what happened just before he took his life?"

"He had come to the house in the early afternoon. He talked to me for a bit, trying to cheer me up, and then gave me something to make me sleep. When I woke up hours later, he was already dead and had been carried away."

"Did anyone see him fall from the window?"

"My nurse. She had gone to get a breath of fresh air when Luther came in to see me. He had promised to stay with me until she returned."

"Could someone have killed your father and the doctor?"

Autumn slowly shook her head, "No, I don't believe so. The official pronouncement both times was suicide. As far as I know neither man had any enemies. So why would anyone want to kill them?"

"But you said both men had every reason to want to live."

Suddenly Autumn turned her face away, and her voice grew bitter and harsh. "Maybe I am a black widow, like Sherman told me once when he was mad at me. I have always felt that secretly they all — Mother, Sherman, Audra, and even Dr. Marler — secretly think I was someway responsible for my father's and Dr. Reisner's deaths even though the coroner's verdict in both cases was suicide."

"You can't dwell on such ideas," Max urged.

Autumn picked up the roll and nibbled at it absently. "I think a lot of things and all of them are crazy, I suppose. I sometimes wonder if I *am* deranged."

"No. Don't ever consider such a thing!" Max protested.

But a hornet of alarm was fluttering wildly inside his head. What if Autumn was unbalanced, perhaps a dual personality who did terrible deeds that were hidden from the sweet, gentle part of her nature? He had heard of such things.

"Max, I'm going to tell you something. And you may really think I'm crazy when I tell you this." Laying down the roll, Autumn leaned toward Max. "My house has an evil feel to it. You will think I'm imagining things — and I probably am. But sometimes I awake in the night, and I seem to sense that evil things are taking place around me. And for some time now, I have heard hurried footsteps in the halls and strange sounding talk — in whispers, but not English — or Spanish."

Max started to speak but she rushed on. "Twice I have awakened and known someone was in my room. Whoever it was would not speak when I called out in alarm. I could vaguely see a dark figure in the shadows, and I could feel its eyes upon me. I heard breathing, but it wouldn't say a word even when I threatened to scream. The first time I did scream. There was a soft rustle, and I saw an indistinct figure, draped in a long dark robe, slip out into the darkened hall."

"Did you tell someone about that?"

"Yes, I told everyone, but they hooted and said it was just a nightmare. They think I'm neurotic, even Dr. Marler. No one takes me seriously in my house."

Autumn sighed. "The only time I ever felt like I was a real person was when I was acting or singing. Maybe that was why I loved it. People acted like they loved and appreciated me, and I felt alive and useful and wonderful! Do you think that was vain, Max?"

Sudden steps on the stone walk out in the patio caused them both to turn their heads. A slightly stooped, thin man and Audra were walking quickly toward them.

Autumn jumped to her feet like a guilty child. "They've discovered my absence! I've stayed too long," she said in a panic-edged voice.

"Autumn!" Max said sharply. "You're an adult! Do you have to account for your actions like a naughty kid?"

Autumn turned surprised eyes toward Max, then she looked again at her sister and the thin man bearing down upon them. Max saw her suddenly straighten her shoulders and lift her head slightly.

The two intruders stopped at the edge of the gallery. Audra, her back ramrod straight and her angular face set in stark lines of disapproval spoke first. "Autumn, how could you? You had us worried half to death! Traipsing around in the middle of the night — anything could happen to you!"

Max felt his ire rise. He spoke calmly but firmly. "Nothing could happen to Mrs. Caldwell over here, ma'am."

Audra threw him an enraged glance. "We don't know that!"

She turned back to Autumn. "We searched the house over! You could have passed out somewhere for all we knew. You could have been considerate enough to let us know you were going over to the neighbors to visit their chauffeur!"

The way she said the word "chauffeur" made the blood rush to Max's face, but he clenched his hands and clamped his teeth together to stop the words that boiled up inside him.

For one tense moment Autumn looked Audra full in the face and said nothing. Audra returned her stare for a moment, and then a slight flush rose in her stern cheeks and she dropped her gaze. She turned toward the man who stood by watching the little drama with an expressionless face. "Dr. Marler, you tell her how upset we have been."

Dr. Marler raised a thin hand to wipe his bald head with a white handkerchief before answering. Max wondered if he was ill, himself; he was so thin and pale.

The blue eyes that he turned on Autumn were alert and intelligent, though, and his voice was kind. "Audra's right, dear, you have caused quite a commotion. Now come on like a good girl and go to bed. I'll give you something to make you sleep."

"I don't want a sleeping pill," Autumn said sharply. "I spend most of my time sleeping now!"

"Don't be childish," Audra snapped. "You should be ashamed of yourself! Coming out here to see this — man."

A flush rose in Autumn's face, but she lifted her head a trifle higher. "You make even innocent things look evil, Audra," she said. "Now, go back home and I'll be there in a few minutes."

Audra snapped her jaws shut angrily. With a withering look at Max, she snapped, "You're responsible for my sister acting like this! If she catches pneumonia from the night air, it will be your fault!"

Turning on her heel like a soldier, she commanded, "Let's go, Laurence." She went off muttering, "Why I bother, I'll never know. She certainly doesn't appreciate it!"

Dr. Marler hesitated for a minute and seemed about to say more. The doctor's lips twitched as his eyes flicked first to Autumn and then to Max. Then, with a slight bow, he turned to follow Audra back along the walk and through the high gate without a backward glance.

Autumn suddenly threw back her head and laughed triumphantly. "I didn't know I had it in me! Thanks, Max!"

Just as quickly, though, she sobered. "But it isn't a real victory. I know what will happen now. Dr. Marler will insist on giving me a shot, and I'll sleep for two days and be listless for two more. It happens anytime the family decrees I have over-exerted myself. I really can't win," she said dispiritedly.

"Can't you refuse to take medication that knocks you out so completely?" Max asked.

"I could, but in the end they always wear me down and I give in. If I absolutely refuse to be sedated, they appeal to Mother. And I can't stand up to her." There was a tremor in Autumn's voice. "She cries and looks so-so pitiful, I-I always give in."

Suddenly she laughed, but a quiver belied its mirthfulness. "I'm sorry; I'm being a complete baby. Crying on your shoulder and acting like my family are monsters.

They're just trying to take care of me. And it must be frustrating when they feel I'm not cooperative. They do mean well, Max, really they do. I should be grateful and I usually am, but lately I can't seem to put anything in proper perspective!"

She held out a slim hand to Max. "Good night, and thank you for being so kind. I feel so much stronger than when I came over, especially in spirit."

"My pleasure," Max said gently as he covered her hand with his and pressed it. "I'll walk you to your door." Taking her arm, he guided her down the walk.

"Do you like flowers?" Autumn asked as they neared the gate.

"Very much."

"When I feel like it and you have the time, I would like you to see my rose garden. I had Jorge plant it, but I picked out most of the roses. There are some gorgeous ones blooming right now."

"Just send Jorge over when you feel well enough," Max said. "I'd love to see them."

They passed through the gate and Max walked with her to her door.

"Good night, Max," Autumn said. For a moment her grey-blue eyes studied Max's face, then she said softly, "You have a strength and serenity that somehow fills me whenever I'm with you. Thanks for talking to me."

A warm smile lighted her lovely face as she turned and walked slowly across the gallery, her tall figure graceful in its bright yellow Mexican dress. The light glistened on her dark red hair as she passed from sight inside.

8

When Max returned to the house, Skye and Joy were standing in the hall doorway leading into the *corredore*. He ambled over to them.

"Did you have a nice evening?" he asked.

"Yes, a delightful evening, Max," Joy said. She moved out onto the gallery and sank down onto a chair. "The Garcias were so patient with my stumbling Spanish and spoke very slowly so I could understand at least some of what they said."

She sighed. "I wish I were learning as fast as you are, Max."

Max's smile reflected his pleasure. "I've got a long way to go, too, but I'm learning."

"You should have heard him bargain at the market the other day," Joy told Skye. "I was green with envy!"

Skye grinned impishly as he walked to a small straight chair which he turned around and straddled. "The better Max gets at bargaining, the more money he saves us!"

"You'll have to admit that my Spanish saved us some money the other day at the gas station," Max said jauntily.

Joy asked in a quizzical tone, "What happened?"

Skye looked somewhat sheepish. "I should have tumbled a long time ago that the gas attendants have been cheating us. The rascals! We've been trading at that station for a long time!

"I had been wondering why the station wagon was getting such poor mileage. It doesn't get good mileage but it's never been this bad! Max heard the gas attendant tell his buddy in Spanish to get between Max and the gas pump meter. Max spoke to the extra attendant in Spanish and told him to move aside so he could see the meter. He did so reluctantly, and Max saw they hadn't run the pump all the way back. They have been cheating us all along!"

"I told Jorge about that trick, and he said that isn't the only one that's used," Max said. "He said they can jiggle the meter and make it jump ahead, and use other little tricks as well."

"I think I'll have you take me to do some shopping tomorrow, Max," Joy said. "I want to get some gifts for Mitzie, Terry, and some friends."

"Yes, ma'am. I always like the chance to use my Spanish," Max said. "And bargaining is right down my alley, too." He patted his left-hand shirt pocket and laughed. "And this little ole calculator keeps 'em honest when they figure my bill."

"I want to get some things for Carole's and David's baby, too," Joy told Skye.

Max's eyes opened wide in surprise. "Are Carole and David having a baby?" He knew their intense desire for one.

"Yes, at long last," Joy said, her blue eyes sparkling with pleasure. "They are so excited. It's not due for several more months, but she is already buying out the stores. That'll be the best dressed baby in the country!"

Skye grinned suddenly, abruptly changing the subject. "Max, I see you had a visitor."

"Yes, we saw you walking a gorgeous red-head to her door," Joy said. "Do you suppose she would come over for coffee or a meal sometime, if we invited her? I'm dying to meet Autumn Caldwell, the stage star, aren't you, Skye?"

"Sure, invite her anytime," Skye said. He looked directly at Max. "I told Joy what we had learned about Autumn, Max. I hope you don't mind. But since we live so close to her, I thought Joy should know whatever we find out. I haven't heard whether there were suspicions of her involvement in other deaths as her brother intimated."

"There's no need to find out if it's true," Max said. "Autumn told me herself that three other men she was close to have died." He told them briefly what Autumn had related about the deaths of her teen-age boyfriend, her father, husband, and doctor.

"That poor girl!" Joy exclaimed. "What terrible mental pain she has suffered and now to be dying when she is still so young and lovely."

"Yes," Skye said thoughtfully, "she is to be pitied. However, she may be a psychopathic killer, and if she is, she is extremely dangerous. We mustn't forget that she was probably the one who drugged Max." He seemed deep in thought for a moment, then spoke abruptly. "Max, did Autumn say if the psychiatrists suspected she might be a split personality?"

Max felt dread sweep through him. He had thought it possible, too, but to hear it spoken aloud seemed to give it more credence. He shuddered. "No, but she didn't give any details of her time in the mental hospital — only that it was a terrible, frightening place."

"I'd like to contact that hospital," Skye said. "Do you object, Max?"

"No-no, go ahead," Max said. "But it

87

doesn't seem possible that Autumn could be anything other than what she seems: sweet, honest, and painfully lonely."

"She's also a very talented actress," Skye reminded Max.

Max shook his head in disbelief. "She might do something truly bad in a state of mental delusion, but I could never believe she would commit evil consciously and then act so innocent."

"Now, wait a minute, Max," Skye said, lifting an imploring hand, "I'm not saying she is guilty of anything — beyond what we already know to be a fact — or if she is, that she did it purposefully. But I do think we should investigate every possibility. For one thing, even her brother seems to think she is dangerous — to the ones she likes the most. And, Max, she seems to like you. That's what concerns me."

"It won't hurt to find out all we can about Autumn from the hospital, Max," Joy said gently. "I'm with you, I can't imagine that beautiful girl harming you, but if she is dangerous, we need to know. You especially need to know, since you are the one she has contact with. If she drugged you — and it sounds like she did — she must be a very mixed-up lady."

For a long moment, Max studied the

stubby tips of his fingers as if they contained some important answers and then he looked up and said earnestly, "Whatever Autumn has done — or hasn't done — she still needs a friend. I needed Carole and David's friendship when I was in prison. You both gave me your friendship when you knew what wrongs I had done. I want to be that friend who will be there for Autumn when she needs me."

He hesitated and then finished softly, "Autumn is dying and no one should die without first having the chance to know Jesus Christ as Savior. This may seem crazy to you both, but Autumn has become very special to me. I haven't done too well so far, but I plan to try to introduce her to Jesus Christ. We might not be able to help Autumn, but God can."

9

Early the next morning as Max strolled down the rough stone path toward the wrought iron gate, he recalled Autumn's words of the night before: that she would no doubt be heavily sedated and confined for at least a couple of days. So when he reached the heavy gate, he was amazed and delighted to see her lying in the sun on a cushioned lounge.

"Hello, there," he called through the iron grilling.

Autumn turned her head his way, and then came slowly to a sitting position. "Hi, yourself," she called. "Come on over if you have time, and I'll show you my rose garden."

"It'll be an hour, at least, before anyone is up over here so I have some time. Someone will have to unlock the gate though," Max answered.

"Jorge!" Autumn called and almost instantly the little Mexican gardener was limping toward her. She gave him instructions that Max could not hear.

Jorge came immediately to the high gate

and unlocked it. His mouth opened wide in a toothless grin as he said in Spanish, "The *senora* says I am to have a key made and delivered to you today." His black eyes twinkled as he winked, pocketed the key, and went whistling away.

An icicle-like prickle ran down Max's back. Was he playing with fire, fire that could billow out suddenly and engulf him in its fiery, deadly embrace? Skye was concerned for him; Autumn's brother had warned him, and even Joy was apprehensive, he knew.

He shook his head in an effort to dispel the doubts that tried to drain him like a leech. As he walked through the gate, he determined to be on guard — but still to do what he could for Autumn Caldwell.

Autumn rose from the lounge and walked to meet him, a smile of welcome lighting her face. "I was lying there just wishing you would come out so I could show you my roses," she said.

Max felt his heart lurch and begin to bang against his ribs. Even though she was too thin, Autumn was bewitchingly lovely today in brilliant teal-blue slacks, topped with a matching, lighter colored smock-like blouse, belted to her slim body with a braided silver belt. The bright sunlight turned her red hair into a dark flame about her shoulders.

Easy, he cautioned himself. *Autumn doesn't care about you except as someone to ease her loneliness. And don't you forget it!*

"You look awfully pretty today," Max blurted out, and then could have bitten his tongue off in chagrin.

A cloud crossed Autumn's face and a slight frown erased her smile.

Max stammered out, "I'm sorry. I-I forgot that you don't like people to tell you that."

Autumn's bell-like laughter rang out and her smile was back, "Forget it! Let's go see my flowers. They're over on the other side of the *ramada.*" She turned to lead the way.

"Aren't they gorgeous?" Autumn breathed rapturously a couple of minutes later.

Max agreed they were. Rose bushes bearing blossoms of every description, size, and color filled a large, well-laid out garden. Paths made from stepping-stones wound among the brilliant display of flowers. The air was filled with the heady scent of rose blooms and vibrated with the sounds of bees and other insects making full use of the bounty provided.

"Let me show you some of my favorites,"

Autumn said as she stepped onto a stone that led into the garden.

Max followed her as she walked among the bushes, telling where she had obtained a particular one, and holding up a heavy bloom on another for his admiration. There were tiny roses and huge roses and every size and color imaginable in between.

"I guess you can guess by now that roses are my favorite flower," she said laughing. She moved over to a luxurious rose bush. "This is one of my latest acquisitions. This is its first bloom, and it hasn't unfolded completely yet. It is a rare black rose. See, the petals are so dark red that they are almost black. I warned Jorge to be especially careful with it as this is the only bud so far. I want to enjoy it as long as possible." She bent to sniff its fragrance and to touch her pale lips to the velvety, curled petals.

"Let's go and sit under the *ramada*," she said suddenly. "We can see and smell the roses from there. I'm getting a bit tired."

As they crossed to the *ramada* and climbed the steps, Autumn clung to Max's arm. "Sit there," she directed, motioning to a large chair.

Wrinkling her nose, she said ruefully, "And to think that I used to be able to practice at the theater twelve to fourteen hours a day. Now I do good to stand on my feet for twenty minutes. I'm getting as decrepit as an old woman!"

She sank down in a comfortable armchair with bright cushions. Closing her eyes, she laid her head back and sighed.

Suddenly she giggled and raised her head, "I guess you are wondering how I happened to be out so early." She laughed softly. "I made Audra mad again when we got to my room so she went stalking away. Laurence is really an old dear, and I talked him into giving me a sleeping pill instead of a shot. And I didn't even swallow that! I held it under my tongue and drank some water, and he thought it went down."

"Did you sleep okay?"

"Well, not so well, but it was better than being groggy for two days. He must give me a powerful one. And the shots are worse. I'm out of things for several days."

"Do you really need that much sedation?"

"The doctor says I do. And usually I just go along with him. But I seem to be experiencing a case of rebellion right now. Maybe it's your stimulating company," she smiled.

Max felt his heart bound, and he didn't meet her eyes. She needn't know how she affected him.

Suddenly Autumn leaned over and

touched Max's arm, speaking in a sober voice, "I heard the muffled steps and strange whispers again last night."

"Are you sure?"

"Yes, it was 'way in the night. I had dropped off to sleep, but I don't sleep heavily, like I used to, unless I'm sedated. Something woke me up and I lay there listening. Then I heard very faint voices speaking in a strange language — Oriental, I think. And the sound of many feet. It was only for a minute or two, and then all was quiet again."

"You think they came from inside your house? Maybe the sounds are carrying from outside somewhere."

Autumn shook her head emphatically. "No, they came from somewhere inside; below my room, I think. Maybe there is a basement in our house. I don't know. I have been too ill to do much exploring since we came here."

She studied Max with intense grey eyes, framed in heavy dark lashes. "Is there a basement in your part of the house?"

"I don't know. I'll look into it. If there is, we don't use it. There is much more space now than we can possibly use."

Cocking her head to one side, Autumn's eyes locked with Max's. Abruptly changing the subject, she said, "Max, I've told you all about myself but you have scarcely mentioned your life. Tell me about Max Parrish."

"I don't really like to talk about my life before I came to know Christ," Max said hesitantly. "It isn't a pretty story."

"Please," Autumn said softly. "I really want to know."

Max took a deep breath, unable to resist her seemingly honest interest, but ashamed of the story he had to tell. "I was the illegitimate son of a mother who was both a junkie and a prostitute. My baby sister, Tina, and I still bear the emotional and physical scars of her abuse."

Max's amber eyes went bleak, and his voice took on a bitter note. "Tina became an alcoholic while still a baby. Mother used to dip her pacifier in beer to keep her quiet, and Tina was crying for the stuff before she could walk. While very young, she began to prostitute herself, to buy her booze."

"How horrible," Autumn said. She leaned over and lightly touched the livid scar on Max's temple. "How did you get that?"

"I nearly died that time," Max said. "I was only twelve. A big black guy was my mother's drug supplier. I went with her to meet the man in a dark alley. Mother was shaking and about to come unglued because she needed a fix so bad but had no money. She begged and swore and yelled and cried but that big mean guy just laughed at her. 'No money, no fix,' he said.

"My mother went kinda crazy, screaming vile words at him and pounding the man with her fists. She probably weighed all of a hundred pounds, and the man was as big as a gorilla. I saw the man's eyes go mean, and he didn't even bother to try to talk to her or to swat away her hands. He whipped out a long razor and opened it."

"H-how terrible!" Autumn breathed.

"Yes, it was," Max agreed. "I'll never forget it. The sight of that razor brought mother to her senses, and she backed away, clear against the wall, and began to beg for her life. But he came after her, his black eyes as cold and evil as a snake's eyes, calling her filthy names at every step. There was a horrible smile on his lips like he was enjoying her terror."

Autumn's eyes were wide. "What did you do?"

"I knew he meant to kill her. Without even thinking, I threw myself at him, screaming and cursing. He knocked me to the ground with one quick flip of his free hand, but I was up like a shot and at him again. Mother was screaming for help then, and that's all that saved us both.

"Like from far away, I heard running footsteps and yells. That big black dude heard 'em, too. He slashed out at me with that razor, and then took to his heels."

"And he cut you," Autumn supplied.

"Yeah. If I hadn't ducked back, he would have nearly cut my head off. As it was, I was badly hurt — blood all over. That's the only time I ever remember my mother holding me. Maybe it was the blood and she thought I was dying, but she grabbed me in her arms and rocked me back and forth, calling me her big, brave boy who had saved her life, not even minding that I was bleeding all over her."

Max grinned a sad, crooked grin. "There were many times afterward that I berated myself for not letting him kill her!"

"You don't mean that!"

"Not now, but I did then. Before she died of an overdose of heroin, she put Tina and me through pain I can't describe. We had to steal and fight to keep her in drugs and us with enough food to stay alive. She finally cared for nothing but the drugs. She knocked us around and demanded we do all kinds of awful things to get them for her."

"I'm so sorry." Tears shone in Autumn's expressive eyes. "Your story makes me ashamed that I complained to you because my family takes too good a care of me."

Max looked at Autumn's lovely face, but he seemed not to see her or hear her words. "I became the very thing that I detested. Fighting for our very existence, I soon learned that force was what ruled in the ghetto where we lived, and I tried to get meaner and tougher than anybody there. I learned to hurt and punish other people. It gave me a savage kind of pleasure. It was power!"

"I can hardly believe you were like that," Autumn said. "I sensed your kindness and gentleness immediately when I met you."

"Any good in me comes from the Holy Spirit," Max said grimly, although his eyes softened. "My only virtue was my love for my little sister, Tina. I fought for her, got her out of scrapes, and stole to feed and clothe her."

"She was fortunate to have your love," Autumn said softly.

"Tina felt the same way about me," Max said. "She loved me even when there was no good in me. Just as God did."

Max's voice grew warm and vibrant. "But both Tina and I escaped our mother's fate.

God, shining through people who cared, turned our lives around."

Wonder shone on Max's craggy face. "Sometimes I still wake up during the night and for a minute I'm afraid it's just a dream that will vanish like a vapor, that God has done these marvelous things for Tina and me. I no longer need to maim and hurt others to feel pleasure, and Tina is winning people for Christ in Seattle where once she lived such a wasted, sordid life!"

"Amazing!" Autumn murmured.

Max stopped speaking but his thoughts had jumped to his years in prison. The love of God had been like a river of joy flowing in his life there, too. Even in his tiny, sterile cell, his very soul had throbbed with it, easing the starkness of barred windows and doors, and brightening the days filled with physically exhausting, hard labor.

Autumn's puzzled voice woke him from his musings, "How did you ever find out anything about God? In a mission, somewhere?"

Max laughed. "No, from Carole Loring, a wealthy young woman I was holding hostage. As I told you before, I was a jewel thief, and my buddy and I had just pulled off a big robbery. Along the way to escape, we took Carole hostage. Later, when I was in jail, this Carole and her husband, David, came to visit me and wanted to help me — and Tina."

His strange amber eyes glowed as he chuckled, "I actually insulted that lovely lady and told her to get lost. But, eventually, through them, Tina, and others, I gave my heart to Christ in jail, and I have never been the same since!"

He paused and his rugged face registered awe. "Can you believe that Carole Loring and Mrs. Windthorn's father, who I also held hostage and treated badly, both testified *for* me instead of against me when my case came to trial? And Carole and her husband made bail for me before the trial! Talk about Christianity in action!"

"But you were sent to prison?"

"Yes, in spite of their help I was given thirty years on three charges: robbery, assault with a deadly weapon, and kidnapping. However, the judge ruled that the three ten year terms could be served concurrently. But that still meant I should have served three to five years and then faced a parole board."

"But you didn't?"

"No, only three years. There was an incident at the prison. A guard was attacked by an inmate with a knife. I jumped in and saved the guard's life. That and my good record enabled the Windthorns and Lorings to convince the governor to pardon me. He was a friend of theirs, and they promised him I would have a job waiting when I got out. If they hadn't . . . well, . . . after helping the guard, it's doubtful I'd have lived long enough to face a parole board."

"How marvelous!"

"It was a miracle of God," Max declared. "Parole would have meant years of supervision. But because of the pardon, I'm free today. I didn't deserve it, but I thank God every day and try to live up to the trust He and my friends have put in me," he finished humbly.

"Your friends seem to be unusual people."

"They are," Max said fervently. "I never forget how blessed I am. I never had such friends before and Jesus Christ is responsible for it all. I have peace in my heart, forgiveness from God for the horrible things I used to do, and even a terrific job where I'm trusted!"

A longing filled Autumn's face. "I knew when I first met you that you were different from anyone I had ever known. I wish I could have what you have."

Max felt his heart lunge inside his chest.

He had led some men to Christ in prison, but could he say the right words to lead this beautiful, dying woman to God? His voice was husky with emotion, "You *can* know God's peace and forgiveness, Autumn."

Sudden tears showed in her eyes. "I've longed for peace but it has always escaped me. But God would never forgive me. You've forgotten, Max. I'm a murderer. I-I killed my own husband."

"I hurt many people, Autumn, not just one. It wasn't my fault they survived. But God, in His great mercy, forgave me and made me into a new man."

Max leaned toward Autumn, his yellow eyes glowing. "I can't describe the joy it is to know that I'm free! Free from the demonic desire to hurt and bruise and torment other people. Free from my own evil desires. Free to love and be loved. Autumn, you can know the joy of forgiveness, too."

"How?" she said simply, looking steadily into his eyes, tears clinging to her dark lashes.

"Just tell God you know you are a sinner and that you believe Jesus, God's Son, paid for those sins in your place. He was crucified so that in Him, 'we have redemption through his blood, the forgiveness of sins, according to the riches of his grace.' That's in Ephesians 1:7. Just invite Jesus into your heart and life."

"That sounds — too simple."

"Yes, but it's true. Would you like to ask. . . ."

"Well — well — well!" The sarcastic voice of Sherman Cassel interrupted. "So the chauffeur from next door is not only an ex-con, like my sister, but he's a preacher as well!"

10

Scorn curled his thin lips as Sherman turned toward Autumn. "Big sister, don't you have enough sense to see through this cheap preacher-act? He wouldn't be the first preacher who talked pious while he lined his pockets with gullible women's money."

He turned derisive eyes upon Max again. "What's your pitch? Money to support your mission to the poor people of Mexico? Or is it to build an orphanage for the stray waifs we see begging on the streets?"

His eyes narrowed and he paused, then said sarcastically, "Or perhaps you hope to worm your way into the affections of my poor dying sister and marry her! To inherit her money!"

Anger flared in Max's eyes for a moment and then subsided, "I'm not a preacher, Sherman, but I would like to be. Nor am I after anybody's money. I make my living with my hands, and I'm not ashamed of it."

Autumn rose, fury in her eyes. "Sherman, you have no right to insult my guest."

"You'd better get on inside," Sherman

said imperiously. "Your precious son has just returned, and Mother sent me to look for you."

A glad light came to Autumn's eyes, "Oh, I'm so glad. I'll go right in."

She extended her hand to Max. "Thank you for coming over. I want you to meet my son before long. His name is Roycie and he's six years old. Roycie's been away in the States for a month, visiting his paternal grandmother. I've missed him so much! Good-bye for now and do come again." She turned toward the house.

The slam of a door and the sudden clatter of footsteps on stone paving caused her to pause. A small figure catapulted off the *galeria* and ran lightly down the stone path toward them, clutching an object to his chest.

There was a sharp cry from behind him, and Audra burst into the courtyard. Her hair was in disarray; her face distressed. Pausing, she called in a pleading tone, "Roycie, please bring that mask back. You know it is mine and a valuable part of my collection. Please, Roycie!"

Roycie, a slender child, with a slim, handsome face and red-gold hair glinting in the sun, turned back toward his aunt briefly and called impudently, "Come and get it!"

Without waiting for an answer, he chuckled with bedevilment and began to back away from her, holding up a grotesque, antique mask. The black, leering face was carved from wood and was partially covered with a shaggy, white goat-hair beard and hair.

Audra, her face suffused with anxiety and anger, let out a strangled cry and charged across the yard after the boy.

As Max watched the little drama, he had the vague feeling that he had seen the Mexican mask in Roycie's hand before.

Giggling with insolence, Roycie turned and ran toward his mother, holding the mask high. He came almost within reach of Autumn and then, chortling wickedly, he darted around her to elude her grasping hands.

"Roycie!" Autumn spoke sharply. "Give Audra her mask."

Roycie jumped up on the floor of the *ramada,* his eyes dancing with mischief, and sang out, "Let her get it if she can! And you, too!"

He ran across the gazebo floor and jumped down on the far side from them, peering at them from behind one of the large supporting posts, bright blue eyes alight with mischief.

Autumn's voice became beseeching. "Please, Roycie, don't tease your aunt like this. You know that mask is worth a great deal of money. Now give it to her before you damage it."

Roycie held the antique mask above his head and danced up and down in a little jig. Audra ran around the *ramada*. Her face was flushed and her breath was coming in short gasps. Roycie let her come to within a tantalizing arm's length of him before he scampered away again, chanting, "You can't get it! You can't get it."

Autumn walked around the *ramada* and again pled with her son to bring the mask back but he ignored her completely. Audra once more scurried, red-faced and panting, after the boy, but he skipped away, holding the hideous mask aloft in a slim hand.

Max glanced over at Sherman who was lounging against a post of the *ramada*. His pimply face was puckered in a delighted smirk and a soft chuckle escaped his thin lips. He was obviously enjoying his sisters' discomfiture.

"Sherman," Autumn said urgently, "Please catch Roycie and get the mask before he ruins it."

Sherman shrugged. "Why should I? Audra's the one who made a brat out of

108

him. Let her pay the consequences."

Roycie had now circled back near the gazebo and Audra had paused to catch her breath. He paused with his back to Max, who had stood silent and unmoving, watching the little drama. Roycie was now breathing hard, too, but his pale cheeks glowed with color as he tauntingly held the mask out toward his aunt, prancing up and down.

Suddenly Max took two quick steps, dropped off the gazebo floor, and reached for the boy.

Roycie let out a startled yelp as a large, steely hand clutched his arm. Before he could move a muscle, Max swung him around and grasped the boy's fingers holding the mask with a hand like granite.

Roycie's face went red with anger as he tried to wrench himself free and found his arms pinioned as tight as if he were in a steel vice.

"Let me go!" he shouted furiously.

Max retained his hold on Roycie and called to Autumn, "Come and get the mask, ma'am."

Roycie drew back a small booted foot and kicked Max viciously in the shins, yelling savagely, "Let me go you old — old billy goat!"

Max drew in his breath sharply and lifted the squirming boy from the ground — and away from his stinging shins — so he couldn't deliver another kick.

Both Audra and Autumn rushed up at the same time. Audra attempted to take the mask from Roycie's hand but he held on tenaciously.

"Please give it to me," Audra begged.

Roycie aimed a kick at his aunt, his face livid with rage. "I'll tear your old mask to pieces!" he shouted. He tried to get his other hand on the mask but Max held him so that he couldn't.

Autumn added her pleas to Audra's. "Roycie, baby, please be a good boy and give Audra's mask to her. You know you don't want to tear it up. That would be wicked."

But Roycie continued to hang on doggedly to the mask, shouting, "I do so want to tear it up and I will!" He shot out his foot and his pointed boot caught Autumn full in the stomach.

Autumn gasped with pain and doubled over, her arms folded over her stomach. Her pale face grew ashen as she struggled to regain her breath.

"Now look what you have done," Audra said reproachfully to Roycie. "Get a chair

110

for her, Sherman!" she ordered.

Sherman quickly moved to comply while Roycie continued to struggle in Max's grasp and shouted, "I don't care if I did hurt her. She deserves it! She killed my daddy!"

Sherman and Audra both stopped dead still and turned to stare at Roycie. Autumn drew in a ragged, strangled breath and raised her head. Her eyes upon her son were anguished as she whispered, "R-Roycie, please don't torment me."

But Roycie shouted brutally, "You did! You killed him! I don't want you for a mother!"

Audra spoke sharply, "Don't you speak to your mother like that, Roycie. She-she isn't well."

Max looked away from the struggling boy at Audra. Her voice was sharp but her eyes held something else. Satisfaction? Gloating? Was Audra secretly pleased that Autumn's son was railing at his mother? Certainly she was not unpleased, if he was correctly reading the message her eyes revealed.

Max's arms were becoming tired from having to hold the savage little boy. He shifted him and the boy struck out again with his foot, narrowly missing Max's knee.

Suddenly Max reacted. Later he could not remember consciously making a decision, he just did what he did. Swiftly he strode to the steps leading to the *ramada,* easily carrying the small boy. He swung one foot up on the second step and deposited Roycie over his knee.

Roycie attempted to bite his leg, but before he was able to sink his teeth into the tough corded material of Max's pants, Max swatted him sharply on his tailored trouser seat. Roycie let out a loud bellow and Max swatted him again — and again — and again.

The first three smacks brought an enraged squawk, but after that the mask fell from his hand and he began to cry. He went limp, sobbing loudly. Max gave him two more whacks and then set him upright.

The enormity of what he had done had gripped Max after the first whack, but he decided he might as well do a good job of the spanking while he was about it.

Picking up the mask, he handed it to Roycie and spoke sternly, "Now give the mask to your aunt before you get more of the same!"

Roycie meekly took the mask and without looking at anyone, he moved over to his aunt and surrendered the mask into her hands, rubbing at the tears that still ran down his pale cheeks.

Max let his eyes slide over the three adults. All were staring at him with shocked, horrified eyes. Obviously this was the first spanking Roycie had ever received! Max felt his stomach convulse. He might very well be in for real trouble!

Audra accepted the mask from Roycie in dumb silence.

Roycie stood for a moment with bowed head, and then suddenly he jumped around behind Audra, put his arms around her waist and began to blubber loudly, "That horrible man beat me! You aren't going to let him get away with it, are you?" His voice rose shrilly, "Call the police and make them put him in jail!"

Max could see conflicting emotions flickering over Audra's face as she looked up at Max and then down at the small sobbing head peeking out from under her arm to see if she was going to champion his cause. Something Max was certain she had done all of the spoiled child's life.

Suddenly Audra straightened her back and patted the tousled red-gold head of her little nephew. She lifted haughty grey eyes to Max and spoke sternly, "No doubt you meant well, but you had no authority to take such drastic actions with our Roycie."

She again patted the fair hair and her

voice grew more strident. "I shall speak to your employer and if he does not properly discipline you for your actions, I shall take further measures."

Roycie moved to stand close beside his aunt. He rubbed the tears from his eyes with a small fist and lifted eager, insolent eyes to Audra's face. "Will you make them put him in jail?" He turned vengeful blue eyes on Max, "Or maybe you oughta make his boss fire him and throw him out in the street for beating me!"

Before Audra could answer, Autumn rose from the chair Sherman had brought for her and spoke. Max saw that her face was very pale, but her jaw had taken on a firm line and her voice was deadly calm.

"Audra, I am Roycie's mother, and I will make any decisions concerning him as long as I am living."

She moved to stand facing Audra and her son. "Roycie, you have needed a firm hand for a long time, and you are becoming an unbearable little tyrant. Max only gave you what you should have gotten long ago. Max deserves nothing from any of us — you included — but our grateful thanks."

Indignation stiffened Roycie's slim body and his voice shrilled out. "You mean you're gonna let that big old gorilla beat me and not make him go to jail — or anything?"

Audra swiftly took up the challenge. "Autumn, you can't mean that you approve of that-that, . . ." she paused and shot Max a malevolent glare, "servant manhandling this poor little defenseless child?"

"*Yeah!* Manhandling me! That's what he did!" Roycie said vociferously.

Sherman suddenly broke in; his eyes wore an amused look, belying his words. "Surely you can't let this guy get away with knocking this poor little boy about, even to keep him from damaging a valuable mask that doesn't belong to him."

Autumn lifted her lovely chin and spoke forcefully, "The matter is closed. Roycie, you can go to your room and stay there until I say you can leave."

Roycie lifted imploring eyes to his aunt's face but she only shrugged and said cuttingly, "When Autumn decides she is going to do her 'mothering' role, there is nothing I can do. After all, she is still your flesh and blood mother."

Roycie broke into fresh tears and ran toward the house. At the entrance he paused and shouted back, "You may be my mother, but I don't have to love you! You killed my daddy!"

For a moment Max thought Autumn was

going to fall, and he jumped to her side and grabbed her arm. But though she swayed, she stayed on her feet. For a moment her dark lashes hid her eyes, and she drew in a long, shaky breath.

"I-I'm all right." She let out a tremulous breath. "I had better go in though." She lifted eyes shadowed with pain to Max's face. "Don't think too harshly of Roycie. I was never with him as much as I should have been and have left his care to Audra. And . . . it must be horrible to know that your mother killed your father."

Her voice broke; she swallowed hard and tried to smile, "Don't worry about the spanking. He needed it.

"I must go in now. Do come over again. You always brighten my day." With a wan smile, she turned and walked slowly away down the path toward the house.

Sherman followed her for a few steps and then turned back to Max. Softly, with a smirk on his thin lips, he added, "Said the spider to the fly, 'Come into my parlor for tea, my dear.' " A mocking chuckle lingered in the air as he walked away.

11

Max stood staring after Sherman. The warm breeze suddenly seemed to chill. Was Autumn really drawing him into a web of danger — or death? He turned and walked slowly back toward the gate.

Surely there could be no risk in trying to make a dying woman's last days more pleasant. "Don't be so righteous, Max Parrish," he muttered to himself. "You know very well that you're bordering on being in love with that girl, and you're just looking for an excuse to be near her.

"And little good it would do you if you fell head over heels in love with her!" he told himself scornfully. "Autumn is dying, but even if she weren't, she isn't a Christian. And if she were a Christian, she still would never be interested in you as anything more than a friend! And don't you forget it!"

But the warning seemed to have little effect on his crazy heart. Just the thought of Autumn set it to pounding like a drum until it was a wonder they didn't hear it over in the next block!

"Stupid — stupid — stupid!" he said savagely to himself as he passed through the gate. "An idiot, that's what you are!"

He closed and locked the gate before he turned toward the house still muttering. Autumn was on his mind far too much, and he determined to correct that.

He was arrested by a voice calling his name. Looking around, then up toward the second floor of the Caldwell home Max saw Roycie leaning out a window.

When Roycie saw Max looking up at him, he yelled, "I'll get even with you, you red-headed billy-goat! See if I don't!"

Max wished for a second that he could get his hands on the impudent child again, and then logic took over. It was good the child was out of his reach. He might not come out so well if he spanked the child again, though it was obvious Roycie needed some correction.

Turning away without a word, Max went into the house to begin his day's work. As he went, a thought forced itself into his mind: Roycie could not be expected to behave properly. He was just being what he had been trained to be by over-indulgence — a spoiled brat.

Another uncomfortable thought chased the first one into his mind. Even though

Autumn loved her child, she had not been a good mother. Her acting career had always come first, and her son could well become a delinquent as a result.

Max was extremely busy that day. Taking Joy shopping, bargaining for the items she selected, and shopping for the household occupied his mind and energies fully. Almost, anyway. Autumn's lovely face hovered just at the edge of his consciousness, but he did not allow it to come into full focus.

Three colleagues of Skye's came with their wives for the evening meal and stayed for several hours. The men retired to Skye's study after dinner to talk "shop," and Joy entertained the wives in the gallery. Max directed the maids and cook in their duties and saw to the comfort of the guests all evening. When the last visitor had gone and the house was back in order, Max checked his watch and decided it was too late to do any studying. He locked the gates and doors and went to his room.

Snapping on the light, he stepped inside and stopped abruptly. The strong odor of fresh roses flooded his nostrils. A quiver of alarm prickled the back of his neck. Standing still, he swept the room with his eyes. Then he saw them!

In a handsome cut-glass vase, resting on an end table in his sitting room, was a large bouquet of fresh roses! Foreboding shot through him. Sherman's chilling warning ran through his mind. Was Autumn being kind — or was there a sinister meaning to this floral offering?

Perhaps Autumn had not brought them. Maybe someone else had put them there, to frighten him. He would ask Autumn tomorrow if she had brought or sent them over. There was probably no evil intent at all, and he was letting Sherman's warnings make him suspicious of everything.

Max crossed to the doorway of his bedroom and flipped on the light. As he started across the room to the bathroom, his eyes glanced casually over the bed. His mouth went dry and his heart began to pound.

Lying on his pillow was one long-stemmed rose. A rare velvety, exquisitely-formed rose of the darkest red. Autumn's black rose!

For a full moment Max stared at the rose, alarm clanging wildly through his being. Then he walked over to the bed and picked up the rose — still not fully unfolded — with cold fingers.

If Autumn had put the flower here, there was definitely something wrong. The thought was eerie — and frightening. The Autumn who had taken such pleasure in her flowers would never have picked her precious black rose.

Max took the rose into his sitting room and placed it in the vase with the others. Tomorrow he would talk with Autumn. But there was nothing he could do now. Returning to his bedroom, he leaned over and turned back his bedspread and sheet — and jumped back in fear.

Spread across his sheet were clusters of black widow spiders! His heart beat wildly, as panic momentarily paralyzed him. Slowly, though, his stunned mind realized there was no movement, and he realized they were only very real looking plastic replicas.

Roycie! The boy's name sprang into his mind. This prank had to be his work! Maybe even the roses, too. Shock boiled into anger. That little spoiled brat! He had said he would get even, and he had done so with a vengeance! Not only at Max, but also toward his mother.

Max turned back his bedding and found twenty spiders in all. The creepy black creatures looked so real that Max could scarcely restrain a shudder as he began to rake them together. Once, when he was a small child, he had been bitten by a black widow spider and had almost died. The clinic doctor had told him he was extremely allergic to the spider's venom.

Suddenly, something moved under his fingers, and he jerked them away from the small pile of spiders he had gathered together. Three of the black creatures began to skitter across the white sheet!

His heart pounding at the cleverness and deadliness of the treachery, Max quickly captured the black widow spiders and killed them. He tossed the dead bodies and the imitation spiders into the wastebasket with a shudder of revulsion.

Then, he tore his bed apart and carefully examined the sheets, mattress, and bedspread. He dumped the pillows from their cases and turned the pillowcases inside out. Using a strong flashlight, Max even searched under and around his bed before he was convinced there were no more spiders — real or otherwise.

"This is a bad practical joke," he muttered as he prepared for bed. "I'm going to have a talk with a certain little boy at the first opportunity possible! And from now on, I'll keep my door locked, even during the daytime!"

Max was surprised to find his opportunity

to talk to Roycie came very early the next morning, as soon as he walked out into the patio. Roycie was in Autumn's patio tossing a ball against a board that someone had secured to a pole near the dividing gate.

Max walked silently to the gate. For a moment he stared at the boy unobserved. Sudden pity surged into his heart as he watched the unhappy expression on the child's face, and the unhealthy pallor of his skin as he listlessly tossed and retrieved the ball. Either the boy was not well or he was seldom out-of-doors.

"Good morning, Roycie."

The child jumped as if he had been struck. When he saw Max, his face twisted into a frown and he muttered rudely, "You didn't have to sneak up on me like that."

"Where did you get all the spiders you put in my bed?" Max asked quietly.

Roycie's face went blank. "Spiders? I don't know what you're talkin' about."

A shiver of apprehension slid down Max's neck. "Come on now, Roycie," he said sternly, "you know you put those spiders in my bed to get even with me."

A frown puckered Roycie's pale face again. "I did not! I'm afraid of spiders."

He walked over close to the dividing gate and stared at Max curiously. "Why would someone put spiders in your bed?"

A big cold lump seemed to drop into Max's stomach as he realized the boy was obviously telling the truth.

Max laughed lightly — or tried to. "Just as a prank, I suppose."

Roycie still held the ball in his hand. To cover the awkwardness of the moment, Max saw it and said the first thing that came into his mind. "Do you like to play ball?"

Roycie looked down at the ball in his hand. "Naw, it's no fun by myself. But Aunt Audra said I had to get some exercise."

"Don't you have any friends here in Mexico City who come over to play?" Max asked.

"I don't have *any* friends," Roycie said. He stuck out his lower lip. "Aunt Audra won't let me play with other kids. I played with a boy once, but he said my mother was a murder'r. Aunt Audra was mad and wouldn't let me play with kids any more."

Roycie struck a defiant pose. "When I get to be a tough guy, the kids will be afraid to say my mother is a murder'r. If they do, I'll bash their heads in."

Max grinned and said, "That's the way to win friends. Just bash their heads in!"

Roycie looked quickly at Max. His lips twitched at the corners and Max said companionably, "Are you still mad at me for spanking you?"

A frown wrinkled the small face. "Uncle Sherman said you used to be in prison and that it was a wonder you didn't cut my head off instead of beatin' me."

Max chuckled. "I didn't beat you. I only spanked you for kicking your mother and for treating your aunt and mother so awful. You should be ashamed, you know."

Roycie stared at Max fixedly for a moment and then pointed through the wrought iron gate railing at Max's face. "Did a big, mean guy cut your face in jail?"

Max's hand went to the scar on his temple and he said slowly, "I guess you could say it was a mean guy — a very mean one, but not when I was in prison. I was only twelve years old."

"Why did he hurt you?" Roycie's eyes were wide with fascinated awe.

"He was going to hurt my mother, so I tried to fight him," Max said.

"Did you save her?"

"Only kind of. She screamed and the police came. But not before he had cut my face."

Roycie pressed his face against the railing. "Did it bleed and hurt awful?"

Max grinned. "You're a bloodthirsty little

savage, aren't you? Of course it hurt, and yes, there was blood all over the place. I nearly bled to death before they could get it stopped. Well, I'd better get to work, kid."

"Did you get even with the man who cut you?" asked Roycie eagerly. "Is that why you were in prison?"

"No, I didn't get even with the man who hurt me. The police put him in prison for selling drugs and attempted murder. I never saw him again. I was put in prison because I deserved to be there for stealing jewels and being a bad guy."

Roycie's eyes shone. "Imagine meeting a real jewel robber," he breathed in ecstasy. "A real live convict."

He hesitated and then said breathlessly, "I'm not mad at you for spanking me. When I grow up, I want to be just like you — big and mean and take what I want from people! I want people to be afraid of me!"

Max walked to the gate and Roycie backed away, but the eyes on Max mirrored worshipful awe.

Max stood at the bars for a full moment, locking eyes with the small boy before he spoke softly, "Roycie, I used to be just what you said — mean and vicious. I took people's jewels and money. I knocked people around whenever I wanted and hurt them without even caring about it."

Max hesitated and then went on, weighing his words carefully. "But, son, it wasn't fun at all. I had an empty feeling inside — always. People were afraid of me, but they also hated me. No one loved or even liked me. And worse yet, I hated myself. I had no real friends at all."

"But wasn't it fun bein' a robber and the cops chasing you like on TV?"

Max shook his head slowly. "TV may make it look exciting to be a robber, but believe me, it's no fun being chased by real cops with real guns and bullets."

"Did you ever get shot?"

"Twice," Max said. "Once by cops and once by another thief. It isn't exciting to feel a bullet plow into your body. Hurting and seeing your own red blood running out is no fun!"

"Where did they shoot you?" Roycie's eyes were wide with fascination.

Max pulled his shirt from his trousers and raised it to reveal a long scar across his ribs. "The first time, I only got a crease on my arm, but when I got this scar, I was in the hospital for several weeks. And it hurt worse than anything I'd ever felt before."

"Who did that?"

"A robber buddy that I thought was a

friend. We were in jail together and someone slipped him a gun. Prison is a scary place because you're shut up with all kinds of terrible people."

"I wouldn't be afraid," Roycie said boastfully, puffing out his chest.

"You'd be stupid not to be afraid!" Max said severely. "Even the toughest man is afraid when there's real danger."

He paused and spoke persuasively, "If you really want to be a tough guy, be a good cop. Then you could help people and protect them from the bad guys. You could be proud of yourself, instead of being ashamed like I was."

Roycie considered, his fair head cocked. "Maybe I will," he said slowly. "Will you teach me how to fight?"

Max studied the boy for a moment before he answered. "I'm sure your mother and aunt would be upset if I taught you how to fight."

He studied the pale pampered child before him for a moment, and then made a decision. Obviously Roycie had never had a man to look up to. Maybe he could do a little something to remedy that.

"I'll tell you what. I work out every morning at six o'clock. My boss has set up a room with all kinds of equipment for building a strong body. If you can get up that early — and your mother agrees — you can work out with me. A cop would need a strong body, you know."

Roycie's eyes sparkled and he danced up and down with excited anticipation. "I know I can get mother to let me! When do I start?"

Max felt a sudden tightening of his throat. Strangely, this spoiled child of Autumn's had forgiven him for the spanking and stranger still, he had a winning way — when he wanted to — that tugged at one's heart.

"Tomorrow morning at six o'clock sharp." Max cleared his throat and spoke sternly. "There's one condition you have to meet, though. I'll not have you throwing temper fits or not doing what I ask. I don't have time to fool with a spoiled brat!"

Roycie's blue eyes were very serious as he quickly promised to be good, pledged with a solemn oath of "cross my heart and hope to die," if he wasn't.

12

Max did not see Autumn at all that day. He wondered fleetingly if she were ill from the upset the day before with her son. However, he had little time to think of anything except his duties. But the next morning, as he lay in bed after his alarm had gone off, questions seemed to crowd in upon him and his skin still crawled at the thought of his narrow brush with the deadly spiders. Who had put the spiders and roses in his room? Sherman? Autumn?

Had Autumn drugged him? Or had someone else? Could Sherman have drugged Max to frighten him away from his sister? Sherman seemed obsessed with the idea that Max was after Autumn's money.

His mind went to Audra who certainly was not wild about Autumn's association with Max. She felt he was not good enough — even as a friend — to associate with Autumn.

"You really are dragging possibilities from the bottom of the barrel," he told himself. He could never imagine the prim Audra as one who would soil her fingers with him, even to drugging him. Obnoxious Sherman, yes, but Audra, no.

Logic pointed to Autumn. As hard as it was for him to accept, she was still the prime suspect. The rose was Autumn's special black rose. Was it a twisted calling card to tell Max she had sent him a little present?

A black rose. The black widow spiders in his bed. A sudden tremor ran through him. Sherman would certainly know his sister best. Was she a black widow, dangerous and poisonous? Was the black rose her special delight because she liked black things — dark deeds? Was there a sinister, evil, dark side of her nature that gloried in toying with her victims until they were drawn into her web, to their destruction?

Max shook his head violently. He could not believe Autumn would have knowingly harmed anyone. Yet the facts were there — she had murdered her own husband, and three more men — all close to her — had died.

Sherman was not a man that most people would like, but perhaps he was telling the truth, after all. Maybe Autumn *was* a dual personality with one good and sweet nature, while the other was evil and deadly.

Max felt a deep sadness and revulsion. "Father, please don't let this be true!" he said aloud.

Suddenly, a voice calling his name broke into his morbid thoughts. Roycie! He had been so absorbed in his musings that he had forgotten his six o'clock appointment with the boy. He glanced at his watch. It was fifteen minutes after the hour!

Scrambling into a robe, Max dashed out onto the patio. The boy had continued to call, and he certainly didn't want him waking both households!

Roycie stood against the grilling of the locked gate, red-gold hair flashing in the bright sunlight. His bright blue jogging suit made a brilliant splash on the other side of the gate.

A handsome boy, Max thought. *He's certainly his mother's son.*

"Pipe down before you wake everybody up," Max called. "I'll be out in a moment."

When he opened the gate — with the key Jorge had delivered to him the night before — Roycie said in an aggrieved tone, "You said I was to be here at six o'clock sharp. I was here but you weren't!"

Smart mouthed kids had always been a trial to Max, but he held his temper in check. Besides, he had a point. "I'm sorry,

Roycie. I didn't keep track of the time well enough."

As Roycie marched beside Max across the patio, he looked up at him with wide blue eyes. "Did you know my mother's goin' to die?"

The callous announcement shook Max. His answer was harsh, "Yes, I know your mother's dying. But you don't have to act glad about it!" He wondered why he had agreed to let this obnoxious child workout with him.

"W-why a-are you mad at me?" Roycie's voice was trembling with tears.

Max looked down and was amazed to see the blue eyes filled with tears. He stopped and faced Roycie, "I didn't mean to hurt your feelings, I just wondered how you could act so-so unfeeling about your mother. Since she's sick and — all."

Roycie stared at Max through wet eyes, then rubbing the tears from his eyes, he said solemnly, "I don't hardly know her. She was nearly always gone before she got sick. Then she was in a hospital for a long time. Now that she's home, she's sick, and everybody says I shouldn't disturb her. Aunt Audra takes care of me," he finished.

"I'm sorry I growled at you, Roycie," Max said contritely, not knowing what else to say. "Let's go get at that exercise."

Roycie's eyes quickly cleared, and he tried to match his short strides to Max's long ones as Max led the way across the patio toward the private gym.

As he walked, several thoughts churned in Max's brain. Roycie was more right than he, Max. Autumn had never been a mother to Roycie — so why should he grieve if she died?

A sliver of unease shot through him. Obviously, Autumn had neglected her son. Of course, her acting had been a very demanding job; her husband had seen to that, according to Autumn.

However, he quickly defended, the boy had been well cared for. He seemed to be in good health, except for being too white as if he spent little time out-of-doors.

But was a demanding career an excuse for causing one's own son to say he didn't really know his mother?

Max forced himself to shrug off the ghosts of old feelings as he unlocked the door of the gym. He knew what neglect could do to a child, and he hoped that something would happen to change Autumn and Roycie before it was too late.

13

How did I get myself into this? Max thought as he began to show Roycie how to use the various pieces of equipment. But he was pleasantly surprised to find that the next forty-five minutes passed too quickly. The child was quick to learn and anxious to please him.

He was only six years old and his endurance was short, but he was plucky and would not quit until Max gave the word. Max found himself wondering why the child wanted to be with him. Did he really want to build up his body, or did he long for a man's company and approval?

A few minutes later, he decided he knew the answer. Max and Roycie were both startled to hear a voice at the door and turned to see Autumn, lovely in a warm-orange, belted dress, standing just inside the door a few feet from them.

Max saw the grin on Roycie's face instantly change to a scowl.

"Max and me are busy," Roycie said rudely and turned his back on his mother.

"Roycie!" Max said in a low but stern

voice. "Mind your manners."

Roycie looked up through his long auburn eyelashes. "Okay," he said grudgingly. He turned back toward his mother but a faint pout remained on his lips.

"Don't mind me," Autumn said, her well-formed lips curving into a smile that sent Max's heart into flip-flops. "I just want to watch, if it won't bother you."

"Well, actually, we were quitting for the day," Max said. "I was about to ask Roycie if he was ready for a big breakfast." He turned toward Roycie, whose eyes lit up as he exclaimed, "Yeah!"

"Perhaps we should ask your mother to join us," Max said.

Max saw Roycie glance up covertly at him before he replied without enthusiasm, "Sure."

Autumn protested that she didn't want to impose on their party, and Max saw the hopeful look that flared in Roycie's eyes. But Max insisted on Autumn dining with them and a pout appeared again on Roycie's face. But he cheered up quickly when Max asked if he wanted to help him fix and serve breakfast.

Max seated Autumn in a little shaded alcove tucked into a wall. Vines partially covered the pillars that supported the roof.

Inside was a round marble table and four cushioned chairs.

Retiring to the kitchen with a promise of breakfast *"pronto,"* Max and Roycie set to work. He first sent Roycie out with a table-cloth and a glass of Emilia's special juice for Autumn — along with an admonition that he not spill anything.

Roycie seemed to take delight in helping, even if it meant serving his mother. Max also had him set the table with colorful plasticware. Roycie refused to let his mother help, insisting that Max had told him to do it.

In a very short time, Max and Roycie brought out the meal.

"My specialty," Max declared as they set out a platter of scrambled eggs wrapped in corn tortillas, fresh sliced tomatoes, salsa, juice, and coffee.

"These are delicious," Autumn exclaimed after she had tasted one. "How did you make them?"

"I helped, so I know how," Roycie said proudly.

"You tell your mother how we made 'em," Max said.

"We toasted the tortillas over the fire, right over the burner," Roycie said, "then Max put in the eggs, after he scrambled 'em in a pan with a little chopped tomatoes and green chilies."

"I learned how to make these from our Mexican cook," Max said. "You can't get corn tortillas this good in the States. These are fresh. Emilia just made them this morning before she went to the market."

"You said you were a good cook, and you are!" Autumn declared, and Max hoped his deep pleasure at her words did not show on his face.

"I'm goin' to be a cook when I grow up, just like Max," Roycie told his mother.

A strange expression swept over Autumn's face. Her eyes rested for a moment on her son, and then she said softly, "There is no one I'd rather you copied, son."

A little shiver ran down Max's spine. Max didn't know if it was pleasure or fear, but one thing was sure: he was quickly becoming enmeshed in this family's lives.

Autumn proved to be entertaining company. As they ate, she had both Max and Roycie laughing with her as she regaled them with amusing things that had happened to her as she traveled about the country in her acting career.

Max saw that even Roycie was enchanted with his mother's talk, and he kept looking at her as if he had never seen her before. The extremely uncomfortable thought came to

Max that perhaps Autumn had never talked to Roycie — not as she was now. She had adroitly drawn him into the conversation and made him feel a part of it.

Is this for my benefit? he wondered. Did she usually ignore her son? Was this only part of a motherly role she was acting out for him? If so, why?

Then Max felt guilt sweep over him. Everything in him cried out that this lovely lady was as genuine as they came! But the thought put a damper on his enjoyment of the moment. Suddenly, he wished fervently that he knew what Autumn really was: a gentle, caring woman and mother, or a superb actress carrying out a role for her own, perhaps warped, purposes. Which was real?

When Max heard voices coming from the direction of the far gallery, he excused himself and went out to investigate. The screen of vines shut off their view from much of the patio.

Joy and Skye, hand in hand, called a greeting to Max.

Max grinned at Joy. "Mrs. Windthorn, you said you wanted to meet our neighbor, Autumn Caldwell. Well, now's your chance. She and her son are having breakfast with me."

Joy's blue eyes sparkled with quick delight. "I wouldn't miss it."

She and Skye followed Max to the alcove, and Max introduced them to Autumn and Roycie. Autumn's smile was gracious and warm, and Max could not suppress a feeling of pride. Autumn and Roycie were *his* friends, and his bosses were charmed with Autumn he could see at a glance. Even Roycie behaved himself. He acknowledged the introductions with the natural grace of a well-bred child.

"Would you like some breakfast now?" Max asked Skye and Joy. "Emilia isn't back from market yet, but it would only take a few minutes to cook you some."

"Oh, no, Max. We wouldn't take you from your guests," Joy declared.

"It wouldn't take a minute, and Roycie could help me," Max said. "You could entertain Mrs. Caldwell until I get back."

"It would be our pleasure, if that's agreeable with Mrs. Caldwell," Skye said, his dark eyes smiling. "It isn't often we get to play host to a famous stage queen."

Autumn smiled graciously. "I'm not that anymore, I'm afraid, but I'd love to visit with you two."

When Max and Roycie returned a few minutes later, Autumn and the Windthorns were deep in conversation. Max brought another chair and refilled Autumn's glass with juice as he poured some for the others. He noted with delight that Autumn had eaten a good breakfast.

Autumn's face glowed as she turned to Max. "Skye and Joy have been telling me of his work as an archaeologist and about the pyramids just outside Mexico City. I have lived here for a year and was not aware that there was such a thing nearby. Of course, I have been sick all the time, but no one has mentioned them to me."

"Have you seen Maximillian's palace, Chapultepec Castle?" asked Max.

"No, is that here too?"

"Right here in the city," Max said. "It is really worth seeing."

A wistful look came into Autumn's eyes, "If only I were strong enough to go see some of these things."

"Would you be able to go if we got you a wheelchair?" Max asked.

A light sprang up in Autumn's eyes. "I have one of those motorized scooter things. You know, I believe I could do that! At least I could try!"

"If you got too tired I could bring you back right away," Max said eagerly.

"The station wagon has reclining seats, so you could lie down if you got too tired," Joy said. "I would hate to think of anyone not seeing the exciting things that Mexico City has to offer."

"But that would be a lot to ask," Autumn said, looking at Max with wistful eyes. "I'm practically an invalid. I couldn't walk very much at all, and I can't guarantee that I won't get sick and have to come back."

"It would be no problem to me, if you want to try," Max said. His amber eyes glowed with pleasure.

Autumn clasped her hands and laughed aloud, a delightful tinkle of sound. "Then it's settled. When can we go?"

"Monday is my day off," Max said. "We could. . . ."

Skye leaned forward and interrupted, "Max, Joy and I are going to be away for several days. We're flying down to the Yucatan. We won't need your services down there since we are being met and cared for by colleagues of mine. After you take us to the airport early in the morning, you are free to do what you like. I see no need for you to wait until Monday to take Autumn to see the sights."

"Thanks, boss," Max said with a big smile on his face. Turning to Autumn he said, "Then we can go tomorrow if you think you're up to it."

"I'll rest up today and give it a try," she said happily. Max turned to Roycie. "We'll have to skip our workout session in the morning since I have to take Mr. and Mrs. Windthorn to the airport."

"Can I go to the pyramids then?" Roycie's eyes on Max were anxious.

Max felt irritation well up inside. He was beginning to like Roycie, but he certainly didn't want him tagging along when he took Autumn out. Not that he would consider this a date, but just the same. . . .

Autumn looked at Max and when he remained silent she said soothingly to Roycie, "I think Max will have his hands full this time with just me. Let's see how it works out and maybe another time we can take you. Okay?"

Roycie jumped up, his face distorted with anger. Tears of rage quivered in his blue eyes, and he shot a venomous look at his mother. "You always ruin everything!" He turned and ran toward home without a backward glance.

"I'm sorry," Autumn said. "I'm afraid we have all spoiled Roycie rather dreadfully." She watched her son disappear from sight and then said sadly, "I'm afraid I have failed pretty miserably as a mother. I was so busy with a career that I left his care almost en-

143

tirely in my sister's hands. She loves him dearly, but never disciplined him at all."

She turned a wan smile upon Max. "I'm amazed at how he has taken to you. Apparently he feels I'm intruding on his turf."

"I think he's just a lonely little kid," Max said. "Perhaps he needs other kids to play with."

"I think so, too," Autumn said, "but Audra said they have enough to do caring for me and keeping our household running smoothly without babysitting some other child."

She rose abruptly. "I am suddenly very tired, so I had better go. Thank you so much for the lovely breakfast, Max. And it was wonderful to meet you, Joy and Skye. Perhaps you could come over sometime for coffee. Our cook makes delicious rolls."

She swayed suddenly, and Max was instantly at her side, supporting her.

"Are you all right?" Joy asked anxiously.

"Y-yes, I was just a little dizzy for a moment. Could you walk me to the house, Max? I think I may have overtaxed my strength a little."

Joy and Skye went with them to the gate. After expressing their pleasure in meeting Autumn and Roycie, they strolled back to the house with their arms about each other.

Max walked with Autumn to her door.

Autumn held Max's arm tightly as they walked toward her hacienda. When they were almost at the door, she stopped suddenly and looked up at Max.

"Max, I just remembered. Someone took my black rose! It's been snipped off the bush. Who would have done such a thing? I spoke to Jorge, but he denied knowing anything about its disappearance. And he said no one could have gotten in because the gates were locked."

Max remained silent, deciding it might be best for the present to say nothing about finding the rare black rose in his room. He wanted to talk to Autumn about all the things that had been happening to him, but not now.

Autumn's eyes suddenly narrowed. "Someone in my family must have taken it. I wonder if Audra did. She was so jealous because our father paid so much attention to me and ignored her that she used to take things I loved and tear them up."

Autumn seemed to have forgotten him as she continued in a low voice, "But that was when we were kids. Surely Audra wouldn't stoop to such a mean trick like that now.

"But it was dumb of me to tell them how thrilled I was with that one bloom. I should have known this would happen."

Suddenly she seemed to be aware of Max again. Her eyes filled with tears, and she said tremulously, "That lovely bloom is sort of like me. It was clipped off before it even fully blossomed. That's the way I feel — that I'm being clipped off before my life really began."

She lowered her head and for a moment sobs shook her thin body. "Max, I-I don't want to d-die. Why do I have to die?"

Autumn dabbed at her tears and lifted anguished eyes to Max. "Why do I have to d-die? Why, Max? Is God punishing me for k-killing my husband? I-I really didn't mean to. I would never have k-killed anyone, if I had known what I was d-doing. Honest, Max, I know I wouldn't have."

Impulsively, Max reached out and drew Autumn into his arms. She laid her head on his chest and sobbed like a child for several minutes.

When her sobs subsided, he drew a big handkerchief from his pocket and dried her tears. Lifting her tear-drenched face gently with his hand he said softly, "Autumn, God loves you. He is not punishing you for anything. I can't explain why you are dying, but I do know that God is your friend and He wants to be so much more. He wants you to surrender your life to Him so He can make it rich and full. Will you do it, Autumn?"

For a full moment, Autumn searched Max's face. Suddenly she smiled, closed her eyes, and said as simply as a child, "Dear Lord Jesus, come into my life and take control. Forgive me of all my sins and wash me clean. I know you are the Son of God, risen from the dead to give me life eternal. I'm sorry, Lord Jesus, for all the wrong I have done. Please forgive me and remake my life. I give all that's left of it to you. Thank you for loving me . . . for saving me. In Jesus' name, amen."

Max was so stunned at Autumn's willing acceptance of Christ that he just stared at her throughout the brief prayer.

When she opened her eyes and smiled up at him, the brilliance and joy in her face dazzled him.

"Is that all I have to do?" Autumn asked.

"Yes — no. Yes. You are saved, a child of God right now. But y-you should be baptized to acknowledge to the world that you have given your life to Christ."

"When can I do that?"

"Well . . ." This was moving so fast that Max could scarcely move with it. He considered. "Well, there is a small church downtown that the Windthorns and I have been helping. They have a baptistry, and I'm sure the minister there would baptize you."

"Can't you?" Autumn asked. "Aren't you a minister?"

"Not really," Max said.

"But why couldn't you baptize me?" Autumn persisted. "You and the Windthorns are the only Christians I know. You sound like a minister. Why couldn't you do it?"

"I-I suppose I could," Max said slowly. "I'll speak to the pastor. I know how it is done. If he approves, then I can."

"Good! Could we do it today? Maybe this afternoon, after I have rested a bit?"

That afternoon Max performed his first baptismal service in a humble little church in downtown Mexico City with the pastor assisting. The church pastor, a Spanish-American from the States, could see no problem with Max baptizing a convert.

Autumn was radiant in a loose white cotton dress. She had coiled her lustrous red hair up on her head, and her eyes glowed with joy.

Dorotea, the pastor's pretty Mexican wife, Joy, Skye, and Roycie were the only ones who attended.

Even the fact that none of the rest of her

family would attend — they were extremely upset with her about the whole thing, she said — could not erase her happiness. She had insisted that Roycie come and although he was there, he was clearly not pleased. It was obvious that he felt Autumn was again usurping his place with Max. His face was set in a very unpleasant sulk throughout the short ceremony.

Later, Max thought he should have been expecting some repercussions, but he was totally unprepared for what happened next.

14

Max had just arrived back home when the phone rang. Skye picked it up, listened briefly, and handed it to Max.

"This is Audra, Mrs. Caldwell's sister," a formal voice said.

"Yes, Audra, what can I do for you?"

"I must insist that you not see my sister again!" the unfriendly voice said into his ear.

Anger lanced through Max like a knife but he stifled it and said quietly, "Why do you say that? Your sister wants and needs friends."

"You are a bad influence on her! Do you know that she informed me — *and* her doctor — that she does not plan to take any more medication. Dr. Marler says this would shorten her life considerably, and she could also be in severe pain shortly."

Max felt his chest constrict. "Audra, I certainly did not advise anything like that. I want only what is best for Autumn."

"Then stop seeing my sister! She never had any such crazy notions before she met you!"

"That I will not promise," Max said. "Autumn has only a short time to live, and I plan to do all I can to make those last few weeks or months as happy for her as possible!"

"Like encouraging her to be baptized?" Audra said spitefully. "She may get pneumonia and in her weakened condition, it would probably be fatal."

"We took every care that she wouldn't get chilled," Max said, even to heating the water. "My employer, Mrs. Windthorn, helped her change into dry clothes and dried her hair with a blow-dryer before we brought her home from the church. Besides the weather's warm."

"Her doctor is very perturbed and intimated that you may hasten her death. Autumn was exhausted when she arrived home. Her health is very unstable."

"I'll speak to her about the medications," Max said soothingly. "But she seems to feel the doctor is keeping her too heavily sedated. Being so doped up that she can hardly think is no way to live."

"Are you criticizing a fully qualified doctor?" Audra said scathingly. "You could be in danger of a lawsuit if you influence her to disobey her physician, and she dies prematurely!"

Suddenly, Max decided to turn the tables on Autumn's sister. "Miss Cassel, someone came into my room the other night and put some kind of drug in my glass of juice, causing me to have quite a strange experience. Last night, Autumn's prize black rose was laying on my pillow, and plastic black widow spiders mixed with three very lethal live ones were scattered in my bed. I think it all was meant to scare me . . . or kill me. Would you know something about that, Miss Cassel?"

For a long space Audra said nothing, and Max was beginning to wonder if she were still there. Then she said slowly, her voice laden with menace, "I know nothing about drugs or spiders, but I do know my sister. I must warn you that the men on whom my sister bestows her affections do not live long lives. You could be in deep peril, Max Parrish."

Max heard a loud click in his ear as the line went dead.

"Repercussions?" Skye asked while Joy looked at him sympathetically.

"Yep. That was Audra Cassel, Autumn's sister. She said Autumn has declared she isn't taking any more medications, and Audra seems to feel I influenced her in that decision, but I didn't. Also, she warned me

152

that I might be in danger from Autumn."

"I heard you say something to her about Autumn's black rose on your pillow and black widow spiders in your bed," Skye said. "When did this happen?"

Max told him. When he had finished, Joy spoke, "Max, I don't like this whole situation. Druggings, black roses, black widow spiders in your bed. The whole thing gives me the willies. Your life could be in real danger. Her brother and now her sister have warned you to beware."

Max stood silent for a moment, then said quietly, "Even if Autumn has done things in the past, I believe she was sincere when she gave her heart to Christ this morning. I've got to trust that she was. She needs me now more than ever. She's just a baby Christian."

"But if she drugged you . . . !" Joy exclaimed. "She's a very charming person and I liked her, too, but if she drugged you, she could kill you next time!"

"*If,*" Max said. "We aren't sure she did it." He turned toward Skye. "I've been meaning to ask you, what kind of drug do you think was used on me?"

"Peyote is my guess," Skye replied. "Peyote and its derivative, mescaline, are prevalent in Mexico. Peyote — or peyotl as the Indians call it — is used by many in Mexico in their worship. The Aztecs were using it long before Cortez conquered Montezuma's empire.

"Your hallucinations were more likely from mescaline. Peyote in the pure form is extremely bitter, and you would have noticed its presence in the juice, but mescaline isn't."

"I still cannot understand why Autumn — or anyone — would want to give Max mescaline," Joy said.

Skye answered Joy. "If Autumn did it, she is probably acting out some kind of fantasy, but if it was someone else, they might be trying to make Max think it was Autumn, to make him stay away from her."

He turned back toward Max. "I agree with Joy. Autumn appears to be a charming young woman, but she might not be what she appears to be. Her family could be sincerely concerned for your safety. They have known Autumn for many years, and you have only known her briefly."

"But she accepted Christ," Max said stubbornly.

"If she is a dual personality, you could be seeing only the good side of her nature. The other personality could still be a psychopathic killer. Four deaths occurred when she was the only one present."

"I've got to trust her," Max said. His amber eyes kindled and he rubbed a hand through his short, trim beard. His whole body bristled with indignation.

"Wait a minute, Max. I'm not belittling your Mrs. Caldwell. She's gorgeous and sweet and I, too, find it hard to believe she is guilty of harming anyone intentionally. But from her own lips comes the testimony that she was the only one present when four men died."

Max slumped down and said grudgingly, "I know."

"Max, I liked her, too," Joy added. "She gave me the feeling that she was as genuine as they come. But we still don't really know what she is, and we don't want anything to happen to you."

Her pretty face was troubled. "So please be very careful around her. I wish now that we hadn't started this business of you taking her sightseeing. I'm frightened for you, Max!"

"Autumn is too weak to be a real threat to anyone right now," Max said defensively. "Besides, I still believe she was genuinely saved today."

"I want to believe she was, too. But we have to look at all possibilities. I keep remembering that she is an actress, a very good one who is famous for acting out personalities not her own," Skye said.

Max sat for a moment in deep thought, then he looked up at Skye, his brow furrowed in deep concentration, "Suppose — just suppose — that Autumn never killed anyone. What if someone in her family — or even someone else — murdered them all, and framed Autumn when her mind was befuddled with drugs? With the exception of maybe the first death — her teenage boyfriend — which could have been an accident, and nothing more."

"But why would anyone in her family want to put her through that torment?" Joy said. "She obviously supports the whole lot of them."

Max thought for a moment. "She told me the other day that her family is not affectionate. According to her story, her sister has always been jealous of her. Her brother doesn't seem to really care for her; he just seems to be afraid someone is after her money. Maybe he wanted her committed to an institution so they could get her money."

"Or maybe someone outside of the family framed her," Joy suggested. "A star is sure to have enemies, other people who feel they should have been the star and not her."

"Is that glass still in your room, Max?" Skye asked abruptly. "I would like to have it checked to see what the drug really was, if it was in the juice. There might even be finger-prints."

Max shook his head. "I thought of that, too, but the glass was gone when I woke up."

"That sounds like the thinking of a very sane person," Joy said, "removing the glass so no one can have it checked."

"That pretty well proves the drug was in the glass of juice," Skye added.

"Was your door locked that night?" Joy asked.

"No, I didn't lock it. The outside gates were all locked. I see to that every night; it's the last thing I do. Someone could have got in from the patio since that door wasn't locked. Anyone next door could have a key to the divider gate. Autumn got one easy enough — and had one made for me."

"Be sure and lock your door from now on, Max," Skye said. "Don't take any more chances."

"I won't," Max assured him. "Say, boss, do you know if there is a basement under this place? I just remembered something. Autumn said she hears strange voices and footsteps in the night, and they seem to come from under her room."

"Not that I know of, but we could look around," Skye offered. The three of them dispersed, but a thorough search revealed no doors leading to a basement. The cook, maids and gardener were questioned, but they denied any knowledge of a basement, and reluctantly, Max was forced to wonder if Autumn had only imagined the voices.

15

Autumn, looking fresh and lovely in tailored teal blue slacks and a bright yellow blouse, was ready when Max returned from the airport the next morning. Around her graceful neck was a gold filigree necklace set with lustrous dark pearls.

"That necklace is really pretty. I never saw one quite like it," Max said as he helped Autumn into the Windthorn station wagon.

"Thank you," Autumn said. "I haven't worn it for a long time. It came from Oaxaco and is the only Mexican jewelry I own. The black pearls are rather unusual, I think. Royce bought the necklace for me on our honeymoon in Acapulco. I felt so festive today that I decided to wear it."

Max felt a little quiver of unease. *Autumn wearing her dead husband's honeymoon gift — even black pearls — doesn't mean anything,* he told himself in disgust.

As they pulled away, Max saw Audra watching from an upstairs window. Her unsmiling, stern face was meant to show her disapproval he was sure.

What he didn't notice was the small, dark-skinned man — with a small gold ring in his left ear — rise without haste from his lounging position across the street, step into a rusty grey Volkswagen van and slip into the traffic not far behind Max and Autumn.

"It's a beautiful day," Max said as he steered the car out into a stream of traffic. "I don't think it will get too hot for you."

"I'm just glad to get away from home!" Autumn exclaimed.

"I expect they tried to talk you out of going?"

"They all but called out the cavalry to keep me home," Autumn said in exasperation. "And I guess they really did that! Talk about an Indian gauntlet! First, Audra had her say: that I would come home sick. I told her I was already sick, and I might as well try to enjoy the time I had left.

"Then she called in Laurence, and he advised me against going. It would be too taxing for my frail health, he said. I told him you had promised to bring me home quickly if I got too worn-out.

"Then they both summoned mother, and she shed copious tears saying she couldn't bear to lose me, and she was sure that was what would happen soon if I refused to take care of myself. For the first time in my life, I

160

refused to give in to her. Then she became angry and said if I cared for her no more than that to go ahead and kill myself."

Autumn giggled. "I suppose I should be ashamed but that clan has bullied me into doing their will until I have had it!"

Max chuckled. "Your brother didn't get in on the act?"

"Oh, yes! He waited until I was ready and coming out the door. Then he fed me a line about being concerned that 'Max Parrish is after your money, sis,' and warned me to beware."

"How are you feeling?" Max asked. "Your sister Audra said you told them you planned to drop all your medications. Do you think that's wise?"

"I honestly don't know," Autumn replied. "I just thought I would try it. Laurence keeps me so sedated that I would rather die sooner than live like that."

"But what about the medication that retards the growth of the cancer?" Max said. "I would hate to see you shorten your life."

"It makes me so sick! You know, Max, I haven't had a dose or shot of anything since the night I was so ill and went over to your house, and I actually feel better, even a little stronger. I haven't always slept well, but it's worth it to be alert and to feel alive again."

She put her head on Max's arm. "Max, if I begin to be in severe pain I will take some medication, I assure you."

"I see your baptism didn't make you sick."

Autumn laughed lightly. "I think everyone is unhappy that it didn't."

She suddenly sobered. "Max, I feel so — at peace at last. I know I'm forgiven. I went to sleep talking to the Lord last night and slept like a baby. I have such joy — and a sense of well-being. If I die tomorrow, I will feel that life has been worthwhile."

"I'm glad," Max said. "I feel the same way. I had so much to be forgiven for that it still seems unreal that God would forgive me. But He even forgave the ones who were crucifying Him. That's love!"

"Oh!" Autumn gasped suddenly, "that mini-bus nearly hit us! I never saw such driving!"

"Mexican driving *is* a little hair-raising," Max said, "but you get used to it.

"One thing I do like. All of the public transportation vehicles are color coded. Volkswagen mini-buses and cars that run specific routes are pale green; city buses are brown and yellow, and radio cabs and tourist taxis are painted orange and cream. It's sure easy to know which one to catch."

162

As they neared the outskirts of the city and stopped at a red light, three boys, brandishing a bucket and sponges, descended on their car. At a nod from Max they attacked the windshield eagerly, swishing it reasonably clean, and collecting some pesos from Max before the light changed.

"That's cute," Autumn said. "Those little guys working so ambitiously to make a little money."

"Cute, but somewhat aggravating when they are persistent and you don't want their services or wares."

They drew up at another light and were almost mobbed by salesboys. Suddenly Autumn gasped and pointed. "T-that young fellow is spewing fire from his mouth. Look, he's doing it again! How can he do that?"

Fire bellowed from the boy's mouth and then he held out his hand and called something. The passengers in the car behind them tossed him several coins as the light changed, and traffic moved on.

Autumn turned around and watched the young man through the back window. "He has a torch in one hand and is drinking something from a pop bottle. He seems to be spitting it out and lighting it with the torch. Fire jumps out of his mouth in a long stream every time he spits!"

"And if you looked closely, I'm afraid you'd see blisters or little scars around his mouth," Max said grimly. "That is probably either alcohol or gasoline he puts in his mouth. It's a foolish way to make a few bucks, in my books! Yet you see it quite often in Mexican towns."

"To think what I have been missing all this time," Autumn sighed. "The people are fascinating, and their way of life so different.

"And don't you love their walls?" Autumn continued. "Mexicans never just build walls. They use the stone and brick to make masterpieces of designs and unique patterns."

"Yep, even the sidewalks and streets are laid out in designs, just like our patio. Many Mexicans are dirt poor but they love pretty things. Flowers, trees, plants, rocks, and brick are used to brighten up their streets and houses. I just wish that would carry over to repairing and keeping the streets free of trash, though. Cracks and holes in the sidewalks and streets, and litter all around don't seem to bother them at all."

A short while later they arrived at Teotihuacan, the pyramid complex. Stationed at the gate were several Mexican people, clamoring to sell handmade objects. Max would have driven on through but Autumn asked him to stop.

"I want to see those clay flutes."

An old woman, brown, shriveled and wearing a toothless grin, pushed forward and thrust a six-hole clay flute — in the form of an Aztec holy man — into Autumn's window. A teenaged boy at the old lady's side lifted a flute to his lips and played a lively tune. The piping had a high, mysterious tone to it, and Autumn laughed in delight.

"I want one," she declared, taking the flute from the old lady, "and one of the little four-hole turtle flutes for Roycie."

After Max had bargained for them, and they drove on, she lifted the holy man flute to her lips and blew experimentally. In a very few minutes, she was playing a tune.

"You have a real knack for that," Max said in admiration. "I haven't gotten a tune out of the one I have yet."

A slight flush of pleasure appeared on Autumn's pale face. "I inherited a natural talent from my father to play musical instruments. My singing ability was inherited from my mother."

Her blue-grey eyes darkened and for a moment she was very still, the flute in her slim fingers forgotten. "Mother used to sing all the time when I was very small. She had such a voice! But something happened to her. I can't remember just when, but after a while she just seemed to stop singing." She sighed. "Such a shame. I loved to hear her sing!"

She lifted the flute and began to play again, the high sweet notes rising and falling in a sad, bittersweet melody.

Suddenly, Max stopped the car. "That's the Avenue of the Dead," Max said, pointing to a long, broad avenue between partially restored stone buildings and platforms.

"It's about two-and-a-half miles long and laid out like a modern city. Yet, the boss says much of it was here before Jesus was born."

Autumn shaded her eyes. "That's fantastic! Real pyramids!"

"They're much taller than they look from here. And there were once temples on top of them. The tall one over to your right is The Pyramid of the Sun. The other big one, at the end of the Avenue of the Dead is The Pyramid of the Moon. Each one has its own temples and apartments."

"Wouldn't it have been magnificent to see when this was a thriving city?" Autumn said. "Priests and officials in colorful dress,

166

children playing, and people and animals swarming all over the place!"

"It would have been quite a sight," Max agreed.

He drove slowly all around the complex, giving Autumn an overall view of how large an area it covered. "The city was much bigger than this," he explained. "At one time it covered eight square miles, but this is all that's been restored for people to see."

"Has Skye worked on anything at Teotihuacan?" Autumn asked curiously.

"No, the boss specializes in ancient writings and, for some strange reason, no writings were found here. However, there are pictures and murals to see. Even the colors are still there, although faded, of course."

Autumn was able to see a lot of the pyramid complex on her motorized scooter. She was enthralled with the two highest pyramids — The Pyramid of the Sun and The Pyramid of the Moon.

"How I wish I were able to climb one of them!" she said wistfully. "Have you climbed them, Max?"

"Just The Pyramid of the Sun. The terraces help to break up the steep stairs, but it is rather scary with no handrails. It's over two hundred feet high and would have been about two hundred and fifty feet high with the temple that isn't there anymore."

"Is there anything inside the pyramids?" Autumn asked.

"There's a huge cave under The Pyramid of the Sun. People think it was sacred to the Teotihuacans, and they built the largest pyramid over it for that reason."

Outside of the two towering pyramids, she became so enthused that she left her scooter in the care of a young Mexican man who came forward and politely offered his services and went to explore the Palace of the Quetzal-Butterfly. She had to go slowly, but clinging to Max's arm, she climbed the wide stairway, decorated on the northern side with an enormous serpent head.

By the time they slowly descended to where the Mexican youth stood by her scooter, Autumn's face was ashy.

The young man smiled broadly when Max tipped him well, revealing one front tooth edged in gold. But as Max helped Autumn aboard the scooter and they moved away, the smile vanished. Pocketing the pesos carelessly, the shabbily-dressed man followed them. A small gold ring in his left ear flashed in the sun.

"I think we should go to the car now," Max said, suddenly aware, as they moved down the path, of how pale she had grown.

"I think so, too," Autumn said. She slumped back against the seat of the scooter with a weary sigh, and they moved slowly toward the car.

An old, crippled man was sitting on a tattered blanket not far away, a crutch by his side. In front of him on the blanket lay one lone Mexican mask.

"Look at that mask!" Autumn exclaimed, forgetting her tiredness in her excitement. "Wouldn't Audra love to have that for her collection!" She wheeled over and stared down at the mask. "Perfect! If I get Audra this mask, she's sure to let me out of the doghouse for coming."

Lifting the mask with gnarled brown hands, the old man handed it to her to inspect. His snaggle-toothed smile held a touching dignity, and his dark eyes were alert and intelligent.

Decorated with bright orange, grey, white and black mosaic, over wood, the mask was truly a work of art. It was the face of a young man with well-formed lips, nose, eyes, and ears. Thick, black eyebrows covered the jutting brow and a glisteningly black beard and mustache adorned his lower face. White teeth of shell showed behind parted lips.

"Audra will love this!" Autumn exclaimed. "Should we bargain with the man or just pay his price?"

"They expect you to bargain," Max assured her. "It's part of the fun of buying in Mexico. He will start out much higher than he expects to receive."

After a bargain had been struck, the old man carefully wrapped the mask in an old rag and then in newspaper.

Max tucked it into a pocket on the scooter. As they moved away, the old man struggled to his feet, crutch under his arm, and hobbled away.

When they reached the car, Max drove to an out-of-the-way place and quickly set up a screened tent. Installing Autumn on a folding, cushioned lounge chair with a cold drink, Max told her to relax while he prepared lunch.

A rusty old grey Volks van rattled by and Max watched it idly.

Suddenly, Max straightened and looked after the van, which was rattling away out of sight. A frown puckered his brow and a little quiver of unease stole over him. Had he seen that van behind their car in Mexico City? He wasn't sure. But the man driving it certainly looked like the youth he had paid to watch Autumn's scooter. No. Deciding that he was imagining things, Max tried to push it from his mind.

Then another disquieting thought intruded. Would a shabby young man like that be able to afford dental work? He remembered distinctly the edge of gold around one front tooth when the man smiled.

Were he and Autumn being followed? Max glanced about him covertly, but could see no one who looked suspicious. The gold-toothed, gold earringed man was not in evidence. *I'm being paranoid,* Max decided.

"This is such a wonderful day, Max, and you have thought of everything!" Autumn's voice interrupted his thoughts. "This cold juice was just what I needed. I must find out what Emilia puts in it, so our cook can make some."

"I'm glad you like it. I should have lunch ready soon, then would you like to take a nap?"

"Unfortunately, yes. Thank you for not minding my weakness, Max. You're very thoughtful."

Almost embarrassed by her words, Max quickly fixed their lunch. Five minutes after they had finished, Autumn was fast asleep.

Father, please don't let her get sick from this trip, Max prayed silently. He kept an anxious eye on her while she slept, and he also watched for the battered van and the gold-toothed Mexican man. But he saw neither and soon relaxed.

When Autumn awoke about three quarters of an hour later, Max's bearded face creased into a grin. "Are you feeling better now?"

Sitting up and smoothing her hair, Autumn inhaled and laughed. "Still a little tired, but ever so much better," she declared. "I can't remember the last time I enjoyed myself so much. And you are an excellent cook! Lunch was marvelous." Autumn laughed. "That's one thing I never learned to do, cook. Daddy — and then Royce — kept me so busy doing other things."

Suddenly her face was solemn. "I remember that Audra would be furious because I never had to help cook or do dishes. Daddy said I didn't have time, and besides, he didn't want my hands rough and red."

Autumn looked at Max but her thoughts seemed far away. "You know, I really can't blame Audra for being mad. I got all the breaks. It wasn't fair to her. She wanted to sing and her voice wasn't bad, but there wasn't money to train both of us, daddy said. He decreed that I was the most talented — and the beauty of the family — so I was the one it had to be."

"It wasn't your fault," Max said, "but it must have been very hard on your sister."

"Yes," Autumn said slowly, "I can see that now. But, Max, when I was growing up I was vain, and felt it was all my due. I thought Audra should understand that I was the most important person in the family. I never considered how it must have been for her, always being in my shadow."

"What about Sherman?"

"Daddy didn't pay any more attention to him than he did to Audra," Autumn said sadly. "But mother tried to make it up to him by babying him until he became a spoiled brat. He has never worked a day in his whole life, and he doesn't plan to."

Autumn wrinkled up her nose. "He never liked me at all and made no pretense that he did. Royce didn't mind that mother and Audra were supported out of my earnings; they made a home for our son and managed our household. But he resented supporting my brother. Sherman never contributed anything in any way. In fact, he expected us to support him — and still does — and he made it plain that he did."

Autumn sat silent for a moment. "Royce wanted me to cut off all support to Sherman. He said it was time he learned to live in the real world and making his own living would make a man out of him. But mother threw a fit and cried. She said if Sherman went, she did, too. Royce gave in to me — and mother — but he was never happy about it. If he had lived, I'm sure he would have finally persuaded me to push Sherman out of the nest. He could always cajole or bully me into going along with whatever he wanted."

They were both silent for a few minutes, then Max insisted that Autumn lie down upon the lounge and rest while he gathered things into the car. "Then we had better head for home. I don't want you to overtire yourself."

"I feel really great," Autumn assured him. "A little tired but not overly so." She laid down on the couch, however, and closed her eyes. But in a moment, she opened her eyes and sat up.

"Max, if this little trip doesn't nearly kill me off, do you suppose we could go see Chapultepec Castle and the Floating Gardens, too?"

"Sure."

"You know," Autumn said almost reverently, "I feel like I'm a new person. I now know God personally; I have peace in my heart, and a renewed interest in things. Life is good and wonderful again. And you, Max, are the one who has brought these good things to me. How can I ever thank you? It's like there was another side to me and now it's gone."

16

Max was drugged again that night.

He had used every precaution, carefully locking his own two doors before going to lock the gates for the night.

Feeling very secure, he drank his juice and studied his Spanish lesson, as usual. Growing sleepy after just an hour of study, he stood up to get ready for bed and suddenly felt dizzy. He grabbed the door casing to steady himself. Alarm set his heart to pounding, but he tried to tell himself that it was nothing.

Climbing into bed, he felt an unnatural lethargy settle over him. He tried to fight it off. Closing his eyes, he pulled the sheet up to his chin and lay still. Suddenly lavender shadows, like pastel clouds, drifted behind his closed lids, and coils of vivid lights began to twirl inside his head.

Max sat up and opened his eyes in horror. His room was alive with scintillating lights of all colors! He knew he had been drugged again. He tried to fight off the euphoria that was turning his limbs to mush and his mind to a foggy fantasy of unreality, but it was no use.

The hallucinations of brilliant lights and fantastic forms and shapes continued for some time and then, unexpectedly, he smelled the scent of the expensive perfume that Autumn always wore. He closed his eyes and inhaled the delightful odor, even more delightful with his drug-induced heightened senses.

The scent became stronger and he opened his eyes. A figure was floating about the room, weaving in and out of the fantastic streams of brilliant colors that flowed and rippled about the room, a part of them, yet separate. Dressed in a beautiful, iridescent robe, the figure was veiled, but had dark, glowing red hair.

Max tried to speak, tried to lift a hand, but could not. He wanted desperately to talk to Autumn — it must be her. Striving to speak, he indistinctly heard himself mutter, "Autumn."

The figure came toward him, closer and closer. Suddenly it bent toward him and the figure's gloved hand lifted the veil, revealing for a moment the face of a man with a glistening black beard. Even in his drugged state, Max knew it was the mask Autumn had bought that day at the pyramids. But the euphoria that possessed him made him incapable of shock.

The form moved away, twirling and pirouetting, its robe rippling and flowing, almost formless within the shifting colors.

Max closed his eyes in rapturous delight. He seemed to rise and float about in the clouds of ever-changing colors and shapes. He forgot the form in the iridescent robe until the high, mysterious tones of a flute came to his ears.

Opening his eyes, Max saw the figure pirouette lightly about the room, twirling and swaying in time with the music. The figure held a clay flute, shaped like a holy man. His befogged mind tried to recall where he had seen it before, but he couldn't hold onto the thought long enough.

The music and dancing were exquisitely beautiful, it seemed to Max. So lovely that he felt like crying — and he was vaguely aware that he was crying — crying with delight.

How long the hallucinations continued, Max did not know. Time had no meaning, but gradually he came back to reality, and the room ceased to pulse with color and shapes. When the figure — if it was even real — left or even stopped playing, Max did not know.

The room still contained faint, drifting shadows of colors when Max slipped out of bed and went to try the door to the outside passageway. It was securely locked. Holding onto furniture, walls, and door casings, Max checked the other door of his room. It also was locked.

Still feeling quite unsteady, Max examined each window even though he knew each one was covered with a heavy iron grilling.

Although he still felt strange and a bit disoriented, Max was again in control of his faculties. He looked in his bathroom, closet and every place someone could have hidden. There was no one in his apartment.

Sitting down on his bed, Max put his head in his hands. He closed his eyes and tried to calm his reeling mind. How could anyone have gotten into his room? And yet someone had — and had drugged him again!

Had the figure dancing about his room been real? Suddenly his mouth went dry. The flute — a clay flute, shaped like an Indian holy man.

He groaned aloud. He desperately wanted to believe that Autumn had not drugged him or danced and played the flute in his room! Yet how could there be any other explanation?

Max forced himself to consider the

thought, and the danger it represented if it were true!

Max got up and paced the floor. "Dear Father," he prayed, "Please don't let Autumn be the one who drugged me!"

Then he scoffed at himself for such a request. Either Autumn was the culprit or she was not. But if she was, he was sure of one thing: she needed help and she needed his friendship.

"I know she was sincere when she prayed to accept Christ," he said aloud. He must believe that!

"Heavenly Father, please help her! She needs you whether she is guilty of this or not. If she is a split personality, she desperately needs your help to conquer the evil side of her.

"If she isn't guilty, someone is trying to make it appear as if she did this, and she could also be in danger. Protect her, please. She is your child now and trusting you."

Max stopped and stood still. He had told Skye that perhaps Autumn was not guilty of her husband's murder, that maybe someone had framed her. If that was true, that person was probably still doing it! Framing her to look like a murderess, and as if she was the one drugging him. Otherwise why drug him twice?

An equally wild though came unbidden. What if Autumn was not sick? What if someone was making it look like she was? And what if she also was being drugged — or poisoned?

He tried to calm the panic that filled him and set his heart to pumping wildly. He had to think, really think. If it was true, her life was in grave danger.

Autumn had said another doctor besides her cousin had verified the diagnosis as cancer of the bone.

"I'm probably getting wild ideas because I want Autumn to be well," Max muttered. "But if someone *is* faking Autumn's sickness, there would have to be a motive — a reason."

He laughed aloud, but it wasn't in mirth. Both her sister and brother had ample motive. Autumn had always been the favored child, so there could very well be a festering hate in either her brother or sister. Motive enough.

The doctor would have to be in on any plan to harm Autumn because he had given the verdict of terminal cancer. And he prescribed and administered all the medications for her. Max knew that a lot of people would sell their own souls for a fortune like Autumn's.

This is all farfetched, Max told himself. *Logically, in spite of what I would like to think, everything points to Autumn as the one who drugged me. If she has been responsible for four deaths, she might just be toying with me. An irrational, warped mind would be hard to figure out.*

"I might as well go back to bed," Max muttered. "There's nothing I can do about any of this tonight."

He walked to the side of the bed and froze. Lying on the nightstand in full view was the flute Autumn had bought just that day!

Picking up the painted terra cotta flute, Max felt a prickle of fear. Autumn could play a flute. According to her story, her mother and Audra could only sing. She had not said anyone else but herself had inherited the ability to play musical instruments.

Was she a black widow? Was she playing out some weird fantasy with him before she moved in for the kill?

A deep foreboding swept over him. Autumn was so beautiful — and sweet — and she had wound herself right into his heart. Pain, like an agonizing physical hurt, threatened to overwhelm him. He had not meant to fall in love with anyone — especially with this gorgeous stage star — but if this wasn't love, he knew he would never know it.

"I love her, and she is probably a multiple murderess and a mental case as well," he groaned in deep despair. He wondered dully if he could bear it if she were proven to be those things.

Miserably, he recalled feeling noble and telling Skye that he meant to be Autumn's friend in order to help her. He still would be her friend, regardless of what she was, but he had not known that it could mean such pain to himself.

He knew that Skye had been through an extremely painful experience with a pretty, but fickle, young woman, and it had almost ruined his life. Skye had been trying to spare him the heartache he had known.

Max put the flute down and sat on the side of the bed, covering his face with his hands. Hopelessness washed over him in black waves. "If Autumn were found to be completely guiltless of any crime, and if her illness was curable, there is no chance that she would care for me as anyone but a friend. She would go back to her world of fame and wealth, and I would never see her again." The thought brought a bleak and bitter loneliness to his soul. "If she's guilty of all these things or dying, I still lose her."

Max got up heavily and went to stand before the mirror and studied his face. "As homely as a mud fence," he growled. He thought the short red beard helped his looks a little, but not much.

"Yellow eyes, red hair, and a scar that makes me look like an outlaw!" Max turned from his reflection in the mirror.

Standing with his back to the mirror, Max spoke to himself derisively, "Even if you were handsome, what would you have to offer Autumn Caldwell, the stage star? You want to minister to the poor. So, Max, what could you offer Autumn? A life in some backward village in Mexico! Unsanitary conditions, little if any, conveniences! Besides, you're poor as a church mouse and probably always will be!"

He turned around and studied his face again in the mirror. Suddenly, he had an almost irresistible urge to smash the mirror to slivers with his fist! He gripped the edge of the dresser until his knuckles were white. Now, Max was scared. He had not felt such violent emotions since he had given himself to the Lord! What was happening to him? Had the lovely Autumn bewitched him?

He threw himself face down on the handsome grey and white Mexican rug in the middle of his room. "Dear God," he cried out in desperation, "what have I gotten myself into? I only meant to help a lady in trouble and now I'm in too deep.

"You want me to minister to the Mexican people — in the villages of the very poor. It would be too much to ask any woman to share the hardships of such a life. I never planned to fall in love because I've known you were calling me to this work. Besides, with my ugly mug I knew no sensible woman would have me.

"But right now I feel I would give up the ministry and anything else to gain Autumn's love. It's wrong — wrong — wrong! I know you must be first in my life. Always first!" He groaned and clenched his big fists until the knuckles were white. His next words were a cry of anguish, "Please help me, Father!"

For a long time, Max lay upon the floor in agonizing prayer. He cried unashamedly, knowing that if he did not conquer his emotions now, he would never have the confidence again that he was God's man for the poor of Mexico. What frightened him the most was that love for this woman had made him willing to give it all up — his very life's calling.

After a long while, spent and drained, Max lay upon the rug, quiet and still. When it had come, he didn't know, but peace was once more in his heart. He didn't feel like jumping walls or conquering cities, but a strong, abiding peace had settled upon him. There would be other trials he knew but, with God's help, he felt a deep, settled assurance that he would rise above them all. He would be faithful to the Lord.

Max rose to his feet and climbed into bed without washing the tears from his face. God was still on the throne of his heart! A smile came to his lips. He would reach the poor of Mexico for Christ and his God would be all he needed.

17

When Max awoke the next morning, he felt a contentment of spirit and remembered his battle the night before. However, he still felt it was God's will for him to help Autumn, if there was any way he could.

The thought came to him that it was unlikely she owned a Bible. Carole and David Loring had given him a beautiful leatherbound Bible for Christmas, but he was still using the well-worn, cherished Bible given to him by his sister shortly after he became a Christian. He decided to give Autumn the new one.

It was a few minutes until six and his morning exercise session with Roycie, so he quickly flung on his clothes and made a cursory examination of his room. Someone had gained entrance into it last night and not through a door or window!

But, in the short time he had to look, he found nothing . . . except the juice glass. With a thoughtful look, he took a handkerchief and picked the glass up.

When Max stepped out of the loggia onto

the stone walk at six sharp, he saw Roycie standing at the gate waiting to be admitted; his red-gold hair gleamed richly in the morning sun.

Max tried valiantly to give Roycie his full attention as they worked out on the exercise equipment, but his thoughts were so full of the events of the past few days and especially of last night, that his mind kept drifting. Finally, after Roycie had repeated questions several times before he heard him, he noticed Roycie begin to put on an aggrieved air.

He looked at his watch and saw with relief that his usual hour of exercise was nearly over. Suddenly, he realized that Roycie was standing before him. From the way his lip was jutting out, Max knew Roycie had again asked him a question, and he had not heard.

"I'm sorry, Roycie, what did you say?"

The boy stood for a moment staring belligerently at Max, then he said angrily, "I guess you don't like me as good as her! You never listen to me!"

Irritation flared in Max for a brief moment, but he forced it down. "I know I'm not good company today, Roycie. But some things have happened lately that I'm trying to figure out."

He lowered himself to a leather seat so he could look into Roycie's eyes. "Have you ever ridden a subway?"

"Nope. But I flew on a jet plane to see my grandma."

"They have a very fine subway here in Mexico City. How would you like to ride it, and explore Mexico City?"

Excitement kindled in Roycie's eyes, and then he narrowed them speculatively, "Just you and me?"

Max could not suppress a grin. "Yep, just you and me."

"Okay! When can we go?"

"We'll have to ask your mother first," Max said. "If she thinks it's all right, we'll try to go a little before noon."

"I'll go ask her now," Roycie said excitedly. Without another word, he scampered out the door.

Max straightened the room, then followed at a more leisurely pace. He was nearly to the dividing gate, which he had left unlocked earlier, when Roycie came tearing back. Beyond the small, hurtling figure he saw Autumn. She was sitting in the gazebo at the table, sipping from a cup.

When she saw Max she waved and called gaily, "Come on over and have some breakfast."

As Max pushed open the gate, Roycie skidded to a stop.

"I can go! Mother said I could go!" He was bouncing up and down in excitement. "She said I should ask what I'm to wear."

Max closed the gate. "Just something comfortable and some walking shoes. Athletic shoes are best if you have any."

Roycie tried to match his steps to Max's long ones as they walked toward the gazebo. Failing in that, he skipped along, bubbling over with questions that Max answered absentmindedly.

Max felt his heart flip-flop, and then begin to thud heavily as they neared the *ramada*. Autumn was so breathtakingly lovely! He reminded himself sternly that Autumn was off-limits for him, but his heart didn't seem to hear. It sounded as loud as an African drum in his ears.

Autumn smiled warmly as they came up. "I told Juana to bring out some breakfast at seven so she should be here any minute. You do have time to eat with Roycie and me, don't you?"

"Sure, thanks," Max said, surprised when his voice sounded normal. "It looks like the trip to Teotihuacan didn't make you sick."

"No," Autumn said, "I'm slightly tired, but otherwise I feel great. Maybe I've been a

190

little stir-crazy and a trip is just what I needed. I feel better than I have in a long, long time, and have had no medicine at all. It's marvelous."

"Have you told the doctor how well you're doing without any medications?"

Autumn chuckled. "He says not to get my hopes up, that it is only a temporary thing. The outside stimuli have given me a temporary burst of energy, and it is not an indication of the real state of my health, as much as he wishes it were."

She sobered and sighed. "I know he's right, of course, but I plan to enjoy it while it lasts."

Max felt a deep sadness. Why did Autumn have to die? It just did not seem fair! He felt a stirring of rebellion in his heart. Why had God allowed this horrible illness to happen to Autumn? She was young yet, not more than twenty-seven or twenty-eight, he would guess. Her whole life should be before her.

Then with one brutal swipe, Max banished the thoughts. Who was he, a puny man, to tell God His business! Sickness was in the world, and it was no respecter of person. He'd leave the "whys" in God's hands.

"I didn't know if you had a Bible," Max

191

said, as he opened a plastic bag he had brought with him. He drew out the Bible and handed it to Autumn. "If you aren't familiar with one, the book of John in the New Testament is a good place to start."

"Thank you so much, Max. It's beautiful! Are you sure this is not your own special Bible?"

"It was given to me as a gift, but I would like you to have it. I have another that I use all the time."

"I'm a complete heathen! Never in my life have I even opened a Bible, although mother used to have one on the coffee table for decoration. Show me where John is, and I'll start right after breakfast."

Max opened the Bible to the Gospel of St. John, marked it with the Bible ribbon marker and handed it back. "I'm still a beginning learner myself, but if you need any help understanding it, and I can't give it, the Windthorns probably can."

"Thanks, I expect I'll need help. And thanks again for the lovely gift." She wrapped it in a sweater lying on the table.

Juana arrived with breakfast just then. After Max asked the blessing, Autumn said with an amused smile, "My son informs me that this exploring adventure around Mexico City is for just the two of you.

Where are you guys going?"

"We're riding the subway," Roycie supplied importantly.

No one had noticed Audra's arrival until she spoke acidly, "Autumn, you can go gallivanting over the country with this man that you hardly know, but I forbid you to let Roycie go with him!"

All three turned quickly in surprise at the intrusion and Roycie let out a wail of dismay.

"Mother, you said I could go!"

"Audra, will you sit down and have some breakfast with us?" Autumn asked smoothly.

"No, thank you," Audra said frigidly. Ignoring Max, she stepped closer to Autumn. "How do you know he won't kidnap Roycie and demand a ransom?"

For a moment Autumn stared at Audra, and then she laughed lightly. "Audra, you've been seeing too many cops and robbers movies! Max works for Skye Windthorn, a man who is widely known and highly respected. Do you think he would hire anyone who was not utterly responsible?"

Audra lifted her chin angrily and stalked away without another word or backward glance.

193

Roycie let his breath out noisily and asked a little anxiously, "I still get to go, don't I?"

His mother assured him he could, and for a long moment Roycie stared at her. Then he lowered his head, chewed on his lower lip for a moment. When he spoke, his voice was so soft that the words were almost inaudible.

"I'm — I'm sorry that I said those hateful things to you the other day — about not likin' you — and all. I-I really do. I was just — just mad."

A faint flush appeared in Autumn's pale cheeks and her eyes misted. With a slight catch in her voice she said gently, "I'm glad, Roycie. Because it would break my heart if I thought you didn't. I like you, too."

When the meal was over, Max rose abruptly. "I'll be right back. I have something for you, Autumn." He turned to walk away and then turned back. "I would like to speak to you privately, if you don't mind."

Shifting his eyes to Roycie, he said crisply, "I have a few things to do after I talk with your mother, so you be ready at eleven o'clock, okay?"

When Max returned a few minutes later, Roycie was gone. Walking over to the table where Autumn still sat, looking somewhat mystified, Max unwrapped Autumn's flute from a towel and laid it and her apple-green scarf on the table in front of her.

Autumn's eyes widened with surprise as she stared at the flute and scarf, then questioningly at Max. "These look like mine."

"I think they are," Max said. "Someone has come into my room twice and drugged me — probably with mescaline. A figure came after I was well under the influence of the drug last night and danced about playing that flute."

Autumn's face registered shock and disbelief as Max continued, "When I came out of it, I thought the figure — and the flute — might have been part of the hallucinations, but this flute was lying on the table by my bed. The first time this scarf was left in my room."

"But who would do such a thing — and why?"

"I don't know, unless it was to scare me. Two nights ago, your black rose was left on my pillow, a vase of your roses was placed in my sitting room, and I found black widow spiders in my bed. Three real ones were hidden among several plastic ones."

Autumn's eyes widened and one slim hand clutched convulsively at her throat. "My black rose! Black widow spiders! And who would want to drug you — and why?"

Ignoring her questions, Max said, "I would like you to check and see if your flute is gone."

"I can answer that now. I played it for Roycie and showed him how to play his turtle flute in his room last night. Then I took mine to my quarters and played it for awhile before I went to bed. I laid it on my bedside stand, and this morning it was gone."

She looked at Max quizzically. "I wondered what had happened to it. I thought maybe Roycie had taken it to play with. How did it get in your room?"

"That's what I would like to know. But undoubtedly the one who put it there and played it also drugged me."

"Was your room locked?"

"Securely," Max said emphatically. "When I was drugged before, I had left my door onto the *corredore* unlocked. But last night I was careful to lock it and the others, too. I examined every window and door after I recovered from the drug, and they were all still locked.

"I plan to explore my two rooms thoroughly when I go back to the house. There has to be a way into it besides the doors and windows."

"The rose came from my garden — my

special rose," Autumn mused, "and the flute and scarf are mine. I hadn't even missed the scarf. What is going on here, Max? This whole thing is eerie."

"Can anyone in your family play a flute besides you?"

"Not that I know of," Audra said. Suddenly her face went very still and white. "Max, you don't think I drugged you and played the flute in your room?"

For a moment Max hesitated, seeking the right words. He didn't *really* think Autumn had been in his room, yet he was not totally convinced she had not and he didn't want to lie.

"You think I drugged you!" Autumn exclaimed incredulously.

"I-I'm so confused that I don't know what to think," Max said defensively. "I can't believe you had anything to do with it, but you must admit that the evidence points to you."

"Well, I didn't! And it hurts me terribly that you would think for a minute that I did!"

Autumn was struggling with tears, and Max felt like a beast, but he had to pursue this. "Autumn, I know it's a terrible thing to ask, but I must know. Did your psychiatrists say you might have a split personality?"

Horror showed on Autumn's pale face. "Never! Not one of them even hinted that I might have a dual personality. That's a horrifying thing to even consider. And I would never in a million years believe I am. My mind is absolutely sound and always has been!"

Autumn pressed her lips with her clenched knuckles to still their trembling, and then continued with a tremor in her voice, "The past few days, since I have not been taking any sedatives, tranquilizers or medication, my mind has become very clear. I have tried hard, but I cannot recall *anything* about that night Royce died."

Her face became deadly serious and her voice grave as she continued, "I've just gone along with everyone's contention that I poisoned Royce. Now I'm beginning to wonder if I really did. I cannot imagine myself harming anyone. I was angry at Royce many times, but never once did I ever think of hurting him — in any way."

She looked up at Max and said in an anguished voice, "Max, I felt from the moment I met you, that I could trust you. Now I need desperately for you to trust me. Please, Max. I need someone to hold onto, someone who believes in me. Someone to hold me up and. . . ."

Her voice broke and tears began to run down her face. "I-I meant it when I said my house has an evil feel to it. That I sense things — wicked things — are going on around me. You may think I'm paranoid, but I-I'm afraid. And I can't even lay my hand on anything tangible, except for the strange voices and footsteps I hear sometimes."

She shuddered, "They were there again last night — 'way in the night. And now you think I drugged you! Max, please believe in me! I *need* you to believe in me. Don't you think I was sincere when I gave my heart to Christ?"

"I do believe you," Max said, and suddenly he knew he did, with all his heart. He reached over and laid his big hand on Autumn's arm. "I'm your friend and don't you ever forget it. I would have still been your friend regardless of what you were or had done. But I don't believe you had anything to do with drugging me, and I don't believe you are unbalanced in any way. Forgive me?"

Autumn's grey-blue eyes deepened and she said softly, "You're forgiven. I don't really blame you. Everything certainly points to my guilt. It's pretty scary. No. It's worse than that. It's terrifying!"

Max leaned forward and said earnestly, "Yes, it is. Someone means for it to look like you drugged me. We've got to find out who came into my room and did that. The figure that came in last night even had red hair like yours. The first night, it wore the shaggy white-haired, old-man mask that Roycie brought out into the yard. Last night, it wore the mask you bought Audra yesterday, and was playing your flute.

"Someone is trying awfully hard to make me believe you are unbalanced and to be feared. Your brother has warned me twice that you're dangerous. Could he be the culprit?"

"I really don't know," Autumn said. "I have never been close to him. First there was my career, and since then I have been ill. But I can't imagine why he would try to frighten you."

"He may honestly think I'm after your money."

"Maybe, but he has all he needs — out of my money. A little to a minister or a cause wouldn't affect his allowance."

"He may be afraid I might talk you into marrying me, and a new husband might not want any of his wife's money to go to a brother." Max felt himself blushing, but he met Autumn's eyes with his own anyway.

Autumn looked startled and then she laughed. "You could have something there! That boy certainly has a dislike for work. I believe he would do almost anything to keep from having to do an honest day's labor."

Autumn studied Max's face for a moment. "Max, I would feel better if you had my telephone number, and I had yours." She picked up a glass and twirled its contents distractedly, a faraway look in her eyes. "If I was ever as sick as I was that one night, I would like you with me. I-I thought I was dying."

"You only have to call," Max assured her. He drew a small notebook from his shirt pocket, wrote the Windthorn number on a page, tore it out, and handed it to her.

Autumn wrote her number on Max's pad.

He pocketed the pad with a grin. "Your number might come in handy sometime. If I have trouble sleeping, I'll just call and have you sing me to sleep with a lullaby."

"I could do that," Autumn said, with a laugh. She picked up the glass and slowly sipped. "How did someone drug you?"

"I'm quite sure it was put in my nightly glass of juice. The boss thinks it was mescaline. The first time it happened, the glass was gone when I woke up. But this time it was still in my room. I plan to send it over to a friend of Mr. Windthorn's who can analyze it and tell me what was in it."

Autumn suddenly set her glass down, a frown creasing her smooth brow. Laying her hand on Max's arm, she said, "Max, be careful. If frightening you doesn't work, whoever did this might take more drastic measures."

18

Max left Autumn with the promise to return at eleven o'clock for Roycie. "I know a clean little stand where we can get good hot dogs. So don't feed him lunch. Does he like hot dogs?"

"Loves them! And thanks, Max, for taking time for him. I'm amazed at how he has taken to you." She crinkled her nose and said, with laughter in her eyes, "Even after you 'beat' him!"

Max grinned but said earnestly, "I think kids need discipline to feel secure and loved. I don't approve of beatings, like I used to get, but kids need to know how far they can go, and if they step over the line, they should be made to pay for their own actions. It's the only way they learn self-discipline."

Autumn said quickly, "I think you are right." She looked down at her hands and said sorrowfully, "I have been a poor parent, at best, and Audra has been no better. I'm frightened that Roycie will turn out to be like my brother. Good for absolutely nothing, and grow up with the attitude that the world should cater to his every whim!"

"God will give you wisdom, if you ask," Max said comfortingly. "And there are a lot of guidelines in the Bible to help a parent. Roycie's a fine boy. Give him lots of love, tempered with firmness, and I think he'll do you proud."

Max returned to his apartment and searched the two rooms thoroughly but could find no sign of a hidden entryway. He even talked to Emilia the cook, and the maid Isabel, but neither knew of a secret door into his room or any other place in the house. He could tell that they obviously thought he was a little *loco* for thinking there might be one.

Feeling somewhat deflated, Max dug out the juice glass from where he had hidden it and put it in a small box, and then in a plastic bag, and tied the top.

Carrying it with him, he went into the hall and called Skye's friend, Dr. Otero. The medical doctor had been to the Windthorn house several times because he and Skye shared a common passion, archaeology. Although with Dr. Otero, it was only a hobby.

"Drop it by my office, and I'll find out what the drug was," Dr. Otero said, after Max had told him briefly what had happened. "Skye is right; it sounds like mescaline. I should know in a day or so. Do you know who gave it to you?"

"No. And I have no idea why either."

Roycie, eager and impatient, was ready when Max called for him at eleven. They went downtown in a taxi, and Max dropped the juice glass off at Dr. Otero's office enroute to the subway.

Roycie was enthralled with the swift subway. After they disembarked, Max took him to a little outdoor stand where Max had eaten several times before. They sat on benches in a park nearby, sipped bottled soft drinks and filled up on hot dogs, feeding the scraps that remained to bright-eyed pigeons.

Neither he nor Roycie had any reason to notice the young Mexican man who slouched on a nearby park bench not far away, seemingly fast asleep, with a newspaper covering his shaggy black head. A parting of brown lips would have revealed a gold edged tooth, and his left ear bore a small gold ring.

After eating, Max and Roycie strolled through a large market with little booths containing all kinds of wares, both manufactured and handmade. Roycie bought little shell and wood trinkets for his mother, aunt, and uncle and a tiny, wooden donkey keychain for Max.

Roycie was fascinated with everything. "I never get to go to town," he said. "Aunt Audra is afraid someone might steal me and make them pay money for me."

His blue eyes sparkled, "It might be fun to be kidnapped! Would you rescue me, if I got kidnapped?"

"Let's hope that never happens," Max said. "Your mother would be worried to death."

"Do you really think so?"

"I know so! Now, let's find a taxi. I know a place where you can ride on a burro, like the one on my new keychain. Would you like that?"

Dorotea and Eduardo Garcia lived a little past the outskirts of Mexico City. Skye, Joy, and Max had been there twice with them. Eduardo was the pastor of the church they attended.

They were poor and their small *ranchero* boasted only a crowded three room rock house. But they were hospitable and friendly, and remembered Roycie from the day his mother had been baptized.

The place was always swarming with their six children, an assortment of dogs, goats, chickens, pigs and three burros — one a frisky tan colt with a mischievous gleam in its eye. Everyone in the family who was old enough, worked at something to bring in a little money. Even the burros earned their keep as beasts of burden.

To Max's amazement, within minutes after they arrived, Roycie had made himself one of the family. He was on his best behavior: polite, smiling and charming. A little, dark-eyed beauty — Angela, about the same age as Roycie — took him in tow and proudly showed him about their home.

The afternoon passed quickly. Roycie and Angela rode the burros. Max sat on the porch, chatting with the pastor and his wife in his limited Spanish. They were highly pleased that he was learning their language and told him he was much better than he had been a few weeks before. They laughed at his mistakes and painstakingly corrected him.

When Max called Roycie an hour later, he found Angela teaching him how to milk a goat. As Roycie tried and succeeded in getting only a tiny trickle of milk into the bucket, the shaggy head turned in his direction and stared briefly at him with calm, yellow eyes. Then she returned to her grain pan.

Roycie finally surrendered his place to a

big sister of Angela's, who soon had a brimming bucket of warm, frothy milk. But he proudly informed the family that he would do better next time.

Senora Garcia didn't let them leave until she had strained the milk and had given Roycie a small glass of it to drink.

They rode back to town in the Garcias' beat-up old pickup. As they merged with the traffic on the main highway, a rusty grey van pulled into the line of traffic several cars back from the Garcia pickup, maneuvering to stay within sight of it until Max and Roycie got out at the subway.

As they settled into a seat on the train, Roycie leaned against Max and slipped his small, grimy hand into Max's big one. "This is the most fun I ever had," he said, looking up at Max with earnest, long-lashed blue eyes. "I wish you were my daddy."

Max felt a sudden tightening in his throat as he said gruffly, "I've had fun, too."

A lonely feeling settled upon him. The life he knew was before him would not be easy. It would be great to have a little boy like this — even this one whom such a short while before he had considered a spoiled brat — to share his life with and to teach to avoid the pitfalls he had fallen into.

His mind strayed to Autumn. It seemed

to wander in that direction very easily. *Cut it out,* he said sternly to himself.

Roycie snuggled down beside him, his bright head warm against Max's arm. Soon he was sound asleep.

A contented feeling replaced the loneliness. *Oh, well, I'll take life one day at a time,* Max decided.

19

During the next three days while the Windthorns were away, Max took Autumn and Roycie to see Chapultepec Castle, Xochimilco and its "floating gardens," the famous twenty-two-ton Aztec calendar stone — noted for its accuracy — and the great and magnificent cathedral fronting Plaza Mayor Square, whose foundations were laid in 1573 on the site of an Aztec temple.

Autumn was enchanted with the beautifully sculptured marble lions inside one of the entrances of Chapultepec Castle and with Empress Carlota's luxurious bathroom with its marble tub.

But they all agreed that the Floating Gardens at Xochimilco, a few miles from Mexico City was the most exciting. The ride on the flower bedecked flat-bottomed boats, through the poplar-lined canals was an extraordinary treat.

Music from mariachi musicians, in full regalia, filled the air, giving it a haunting "other world" atmosphere. Aztec Indians, plying the waterways in their dugout canoes, chattering among themselves in their own language, heightened the feeling.

The mariachi band on their tour boat was playing a haunting melody, while two Mexican men sang. Max caught enough words to realize that it was a tragic love song of a young caballero who had gone to war, leaving his beloved behind. He died with her name on his lips, and his sweetheart died of a broken heart.

The singers swung into another song, and suddenly Max heard a new voice lift softly to blend perfectly with the two male voices. To Max's utter amazement, he realized that the voice belonged to Autumn!

Her eyes were closed and her voice rose sweet and pure, harmonizing as if she had practiced for weeks with the band.

The members of the band had heard, also. The music softened and the three voices lifted above the background music, hauntingly beautiful. When the song ended, there was an enthusiastic burst of applause from the occupants of the boat.

"*Senora,*" exclaimed the portly singer in Spanish, "I feel honored to join my poor voice with such a voice as yours! Will you sing another one with us?"

The guide quickly translated his words to the passengers who could not understand

Spanish, and they added their voices to his request.

Autumn's ivory cheeks were glowing, and her eyes sparkled with pleasure but she demurred. "I just happened to know that song. I only know one more," she said, naming it.

"That one we know, also!" the younger man exclaimed. "Sing with us again, *por favor*."

Autumn looked at Max and Roycie who had sat spellbound. "Do you think I should? I hardly realized I was singing until it just happened. I'm not embarrassing you, am I?" She looked from one to the other.

"I like it," Roycie said earnestly, "don't you, Max?" His eyes shone with pride.

Max heartily agreed, so Autumn sang with the band again.

They were at the end of the tour then, but the band leader eagerly urged them to come again the next day, and the tour would cost them nothing, "if the beautiful *senora* will sing with us again."

Although she declined, Max saw that Autumn's eyes shone like stars. His heart almost burst with pride in her but also from a deep sadness. Soon that captivating voice would be stilled forever.

She explained as they moved away toward

her powered scooter, "Those two songs were in a play I did one time. It was so wonderful to sing again!"

"Max," Roycie said suddenly, tugging at his hand, "did you see that man with the little gold ring in his ear? Why do men wear rings in their ears? I thought only ladies did."

For a second Max didn't register what the child had said. When he did, Max stopped and demanded, "What man? Where do you see a man with a gold ring in his ear?"

Roycie looked startled. "I don't see him now, but he was on the boat with us. I saw him at the castle, too. He was eating a hot dog. He has a gold tooth, too. I saw it."

Autumn looked quickly at Max. "Is something wrong, Max? You look — strange. It has something to do with that man Roycie saw, doesn't it?"

"I think we are being followed," Max said grimly. "Do you remember the man who took care of your scooter at the pyramids? He had a small gold ring in his left ear and a gold-edged tooth."

He turned to Roycie. "Which one of the man's ears had the ring in it?"

Roycie tugged at his left earlobe. "This one. Why is he following us?"

"I don't have any idea, do you, Autumn?"

"No. I never even noticed the man."

"Well, we won't worry about him," Max said, noticing Roycie's wide, anxious eyes. "But if anyone sees him again, let me know. I'll have a little talk with him and find out what he's up to."

But no one did and Max soon put it out of his mind.

They were lingering at breakfast the morning of the third day. Roycie had wandered off and was playing in a far corner of the patio. Suddenly Autumn leaned toward Max and laid her soft, slim hand over his big one.

"Max, do you know that you are the first real friend I ever had? I've known lots of people, but never anyone who liked me just because I was me. You don't make any demands of me, and I feel that I can talk to you about anything, and you wouldn't put me down or think I was being silly. Thank you for being my friend, Max," she finished huskily.

Max felt his throat constrict with emotion. "I hope we can always be friends," he said.

His heart was doing crazy things, so he was relieved when Autumn removed her hand from his and changed the subject.

"What goals and plans do you have, Max?"

Drawn out by her genuine interest, Max confided his aspirations to attend a Bible college where Bible, missions, and vocational skills were taught.

"Carpentry would be an excellent trade to learn," he said. "I could help with the construction of churches and native Bible schools, as well as work as an evangelist. Within a year, I'm confident I'll have the money saved to enter school. In the meantime, I'm learning Spanish and everything else I have time for."

Amber eyes glowing, Max excitedly explained, "My hopes are to become part of a program in Mexico where the students are taught the Scriptures and how to start churches and minister to people, but are also taught trades such as carpentry, mechanics and welding. Then, when he graduates, the young minister will know how to make a living, when necessary. They'll also be able to build churches, and keep the church vehicles going and that sort of thing."

"It sounds like a good plan," Autumn said.

"Sure it is! There could come a time when the foreign missionaries will be kicked out of Mexico and America's support with it. To continue on, the churches and pastors need to be able to make it on their own.

"The Bible schools need to have land enough for the students to grow their own food," Max said enthusiastically, "and should be able to grow a crop, or make something for sale, so they can live and learn without money from the United States. Even if the missionaries aren't run out of the country, it would still save money to be used for other things."

"You make a person want to be a missionary," Autumn laughed. Then her face grew grave. "You know, I feel so well recently, I can hardly believe it. No pain at all, and I'm getting stronger by the day. If only I could live and do something for others — really do something!"

A light shone in her eyes. "I think I would like to teach singing and music. Wouldn't it be fun to work with young people? Even my experience in acting could be put to good use."

A sadness gripped Max's heart at her words, and even after they finished breakfast and parted, the pain haunted him.

That evening, he received a call from Dr. Otero about the glass, something he had almost forgotten during the preceding days.

"There's no doubt about it," the doctor stated, "the juice in the glass contained mescaline. I took the liberty of showing the glass to a friend who dabbles in finger-printing for a hobby, but he said the glass had been wiped clean of prints."

Max called Autumn and told her the news.

"Be very careful, Max. Someone who would stoop to such a low trick might not stop at. . . ." Autumn hesitated then said softly, "Do take care, Max. You have become very dear to Roycie and me."

20

Stretching luxuriously, Max stepped onto the flagstone walk at six o'clock sharp the next morning. He stood for a moment, drinking in the freshness of the day. His senses seemed tingly alive this morning, and his spirit seemed to soar with the joy of living. The world was beautiful and he was glad, wonderously glad to be a part of it!

It had rained the night before and the air was fragrant with the odors of rain, wet green plants, and flower blossoms. The trees and shrubs looked freshly scrubbed in the golden sunlight glistening on their leaves.

He saw Roycie leaning on the grilling of the high dividing gate, looking through at him. He opened his mouth to call a cheery greeting when, suddenly, Roycie pointed above Max's head. In a voice shrill, and charged with terror, he screamed, "Look out, Max! Run! Run!"

Max flung a quick glance up, then hurled his body sideways in a frantic effort to escape the huge terra cotta pot that was poised for a trembling second on the *galeria* above. Just as he moved, it hurtled down toward him.

He twisted away as he fell — something he had learned to do years before when he was trying to survive in the street fighting of the ghetto-jungle. He struck the rough stone pavement and felt the sting of skin being scraped from his arm and hand as he rolled wildly for several yards.

Bits and pieces of pottery spattered about him, some striking his body. He sat up dazedly and shook his head to clear it. His whole body ached from the jar of his fall, and his head had a persistent hum in it like the angry drone of swarming bees.

"Thank you, Father, for having your hand upon my life," he muttered fervently. "If Roycie had not yelled when he did . . . !"

His eyes swept the yard and a shudder went through him. The huge clay pot lay shattered in the exact place where he had been standing. Damp dirt, moss, and the flowering shrub it contained were strewn over the flagstones.

Abruptly, Max's eyes narrowed. That heavy terra cotta pot had not fallen by accident! Someone had intended to kill him! A second thought galvanized Max into action — that person might still be on the porch above!

Only dimly aware of the sting from his scrapes and bruises, he scrambled to his feet and sprinted to the outside stairway that led up onto the upper story porch. He rushed up the steps and burst out onto the *galeria*.

His eyes swept the porch that extended in a long, unbroken oval to completely encircle the lower patio like a sundeck. Here, as below, there was a wall shutting off the Windthorn section of the house from the neighbor's portion.

No one was in sight. Max walked swiftly to the door in the heavy, wooden dividing wall. It was securely locked. But there would have been time for the would-be murderer to have used it. Max was sure he — or she — had disappeared there.

Max made a rapid search of the open-sided rooms along the gallery, but he knew he wouldn't find anyone and he didn't. Max checked them all, anyway, and found them all secured.

He walked to the parapet from which the pot had fallen. The four foot wall extended all around the edge of the upper porch with spaces about fifteen feet apart containing large pots planted with flowering shrubs and small trees.

He examined the space from which the pot had fallen. Made of baked clay and filled with dirt, the large pot would have been heavy. It would have taken a hefty person to push it off.

Max knelt to examine the floor more closely, and his mouth tightened into a grim line. There was a freshly cut groove in the painted wood of the floor where a metal tool like a crowbar had been inserted. A man or woman could have shoved the heavy pot off with such a tool!

Max walked slowly back down the stairs. He felt his hair prickle as he thought he would probably never come any closer to death and survive! And the would-be killer knew he had not succeeded.

Fear spread like hot lightning through his veins, constricting his chest and tightening his throat. Before he had known Christ, Max had flirted with death and fought at the drop of a hat, often dropping it himself. Fortified by alcohol, he had gloried in his narrow escapes and had foolishly laughed in the face of death.

But not anymore! Life was precious to him now, and again, he thanked God from a full heart that Roycie had seen the pot beginning to fall.

Roycie! He had forgotten the child!

Max sprinted down the rest of the steps and out onto the stone walk. Roycie was no longer at the wall. Walking quickly to the gate, Max looked through the grilling and saw the boy sitting under a small tree nearby.

Max unlocked the gate and walked over to him. The child sat very still, and he didn't even look up when Max came near.

"Roycie?"

If he heard, he showed no sign.

Max knelt to look into his face and spoke softly, "Roycie, thanks for calling out to me. You saved my life, kid."

Roycie continued to stare at the ground. The fingers of one hand plucked aimlessly at the cloth of his trousers.

Then Max saw that Roycie's face was grey and drawn. He turned the boy's head up with a gentle hand under the small, firm chin. The child looked at Max with glazed, unseeing eyes.

Alarmed, Max spoke sharply, "Roycie! What's the matter?"

Roycie moved slightly and made an inarticulate sound.

Max lifted one of the boy's hands. It was as cold as polar ice! Max put his hands on Roycie's small shoulders and shook him sharply.

Roycie seemed to respond in slow motion. His eyes began to focus, and he seemed to become aware of Max after a long moment. Then his lips trembled, and he tried to speak but no words came.

"What is it?" Max asked anxiously.

When the boy just stared at him, Max wondered if his brush with death had frightened the boy almost senseless. "I'm okay, Roycie," he said. "See, only a few scrapes and bruises!"

Roycie suddenly turned around and began to retch. Spasms of violent nausea gripped him for several minutes. Max pulled out a large white handkerchief, wet it in the spray of a nearby fountain, and put it on Roycie's forehead.

As soon as the vomiting had passed, Max wiped his face with the wet handkerchief. Picking up the slight figure, Max carried him up on the *ramada* and laid him on a lounge.

"Are you all right now?" Max asked anxiously. "I think I had better go get your mother and the doctor."

Roycie shot upright. "No! D-don't get her!"

Puzzled, Max asked, "But why, Roycie? You're acting very strange. Why don't you want your mother? You're sick."

Roycie looked at Max with stricken eyes. His voice was low and laden with misery.

"Don't you know? She's the one who pushed the pot off on you. S-she — m-my mother tried to k-kill you. Just like she did m-my daddy."

A chill ran down Max's spine but he tried to laugh, "Roycie, you're imagining things. Your mother wouldn't hurt me."

"I-I saw her." Tears were spilling down his tragic face.

Without warning, Autumn's words of the night before came clearly to his mind, "Please be careful, Max. You have become very dear to Roycie and me."

And on its heels, he recalled her brother's warning, "Autumn Caldwell is as beautiful as a dream, but watch out if she takes a liking to you! It isn't healthy."

Max felt as if a mule had kicked him in the stomach. It wasn't true! He would not believe it!

Because of his inner turmoil, his voice was rough when he spoke again, "Roycie, are you sure you saw your mother push that pot off on me? Think, now! Tell me exactly what you saw."

Roycie mopped at his eyes with his sweatshirt sleeve. "I was watchin' you, and I didn't see anything until just before I yelled. Then I saw that pot begin to slide toward the edge."

He paused, and looked away toward the Windthorn house. "At first I didn't know what was happenin'. Then I saw the pot was gonna fall right on top of you! So I yelled."

"You said you saw who did it," Max prompted impatiently.

Roycie nodded his head. "When the pot went off the edge, I saw a person scrunched down on the floor of the porch. It was m-mother."

For a moment Max felt like he, too, was going to be violently ill. His head seemed to spin, and his stomach convulsed like the ocean in a storm.

Suddenly he was aware that Roycie was shaking his arm and asking urgently, "Max, are you all right?"

The world righted and the nausea subsided but his insides still felt quivery. "I'm okay."

He drew in a deep breath, "Are you positive it was your mother you saw?"

"Yes!"

"You saw her face? Did you see her plainly?"

"Yes — no — I didn't see her face. But I didn't need to! She crawled real quick behind the wall up there, but I saw her plain before. She had on that blue robe-like dress

225

with all the bright embroidery, and I saw her red hair.”

“But you didn’t see her face?”

“I didn’t need to,” Roycie said patiently. “Like I said, I saw her. . . .”

“Anyone could wear her blue dress and a red wig,” Max interrupted.

Roycie’s eyes grew wide, tragic with hope, “You — you mean it might not have b-been m-mother?”

“That’s a definite possibility,” Max said. *Dear God, let it be so,* he prayed fervently. He didn’t even remind himself that it was a foolish prayer — that either she had or she hadn’t tried to kill him. His feelings were so deep for Autumn that he would not — could not — let himself believe for a minute that she was guilty.

A little color had crept back into Roycie’s pale cheeks. His chin came up and he said, “Then I’m goin’ to believe she didn’t do it!”

Max’s heart lurched with pain. This poor child had been through so much, living through the trauma of knowing his father had been killed by his own mother. Max prayed that he wasn’t in for more horror — in any form.

But, if Autumn had not attempted to kill him, then someone else had and had dressed to look like her in case he was seen.

Maybe the would-be killer had even meant for Roycie to see him!

Suddenly, he heard Roycie give an involuntarily gasp, and he felt the child's hands clutch at Max's clothes convulsively. Max looked at him sharply and saw that his face had gone waxy pale and his eyes were wide with fear.

Max quickly turned.

Walking gracefully toward them with a smile on her lovely face was Autumn Caldwell, gorgeously arrayed in a full, bright blue, robe-like dress, lavishly embroidered in rich colors!

21

Autumn called gaily, "How are you gentlemen today? I thought you'd still be building muscles."

Then she caught sight of Roycie's face and wide, frightened eyes. The smile disappeared from her face and she hurried forward to kneel in front of her son. "What's the matter, Roycie?" She tried to touch his face, but he shrank away.

Autumn looked bewildered, "Roycie, are you sick?"

When he continued to stare at her mutely, she stood quickly to her feet, alarm stamped clearly on her face. "Max, what's wrong with him? He looks like he's seen a ghost."

"I think he has," Max said enigmatically.

"Wha-what do you mean?"

"A person with red hair, and dressed in a dress like the one you are wearing, tried to kill me a few minutes ago."

"Oh, no!" Shock drained all the color from Autumn's face. She closed her eyes and for a minute it seemed as if she was going to faint.

Max laid his hand on her arm to steady her.

She twisted her hands tightly together and drew in a ragged breath. Her eyes snapped open and she said in a strained voice, "What happened?"

"I stepped out on the sidewalk in our patio. Roycie saw a huge clay pot being pushed off our *galeria* right on top of me, and yelled. If Roycie hadn't yelled and I hadn't moved awfully quick, I'd be lying under it now with my skull bashed in."

"How do you know someone pushed it off on you? Did you see someone?"

"After the pot fell, Roycie saw a person with red hair and a bright blue robe-like dress, embroidered like yours, crawl behind the wall. I ran up there but no one was there."

Autumn's eyes were anguished. "And Roycie thinks I'm the one who tried to kill you?"

Her face crumpled, and she dropped in a heap on the patio stones, covering her face with her hands. "Dear God, when will this thing ever end?" For perhaps a minute her shoulders shook with sobs, while Max stood silent, his mind torn with conflict.

The speechless child still held on to him with clenched fingers, his eyes haunted.

Unable to bear it any longer, Max forced

aside his doubts and dropped to one knee beside Autumn. Placing his free hand around her shaking shoulders, he just held her.

Then Autumn seemed to take a firm grip on her emotions. She raised her head and wiped her face with some tissues she found in the pocket of her dress. Drawing in gulps of air, she straightened her shoulders and Max heard her soft, "Dear Jesus, please help me now."

Without rising, she lifted her head and searched first Max's face and then Roycie's. Her eyes were still misted, but her voice was calm. "I never pushed that pot off on Max, Roycie. I know it was planned to look like that, but it isn't true!"

Her eyes shifted to Max. "I always select the clothes I'm going to wear the next day and hang them on a special rack for that purpose in my room. If I'm not well, I have Juana do it. It's a habit I acquired when I was an actress, to save time the next day.

"I laid this dress out last night before I retired. This morning I took a leisurely bath, as I always do before I start my day. And when. . . ."

"Was your dress still hanging on the rack when you went in to take your bath?" Max interrupted.

Autumn thought briefly. "I don't recall. If it wasn't, I probably would not have noticed, but when I came out and began to dress, everything I had laid out was there.

"No!" She let out a little cry. "No, they weren't! One thing was missing! The long sash that goes with this dress was gone, and I thought I forgot to lay it out. But it wasn't in the closet either when I looked.

"But as I think about it, I *know* it was with the dress last night, because I debated on whether or not to wear it. And I decided on the belt!"

She jumped up and exclaimed, "You two come with me. We'll go up on our side of the *galeria* and see if we can find anything. Maybe our mystery person dropped my belt there!"

She led the way to the stairway. Roycie followed but stayed close to Max as if he were afraid of his mother. As they ascended single file, Autumn spoke back over her shoulder. "This stairway runs right next to my suite of rooms. There is a stairway inside my *sala* that leads up here, too. It comes out inside the covered porch."

One glance down the length of the *galeria* showed no sign of the bright sash.

"Let's go inside the gallery," Autumn said.

They scattered, looking here and there. Suddenly, Roycie said excitedly, "Here's your belt, Mother."

The rich blue sash lay on the treads of the inside stairway going down to the lower floor.

At almost the same time, Max called from the end close to the divider wall. His voice rang with excitement. "Come see what I found!"

Lying behind a long settee was a heavy crowbar.

"I thought whoever carried this would hide it as soon as possible because it would be too heavy to carry very far," Max said with satisfaction.

Autumn studied the belt in her hand as if it held the answers. "Someone wore my dress up here to make it look like I was the person who pushed off that pot on you."

She turned to Max. "Do you think the person really meant to kill you or just frighten you?"

"If Roycie hadn't called out, I'd be dead," Max said grimly. "That person meant to kill me!"

"This is extremely serious," Autumn said. "What are you going to do, call the police?"

"I don't know. I wish the Windthorns were home so I could ask what they think.

They should be in sometime today. The proper thing is to inform the police, I suppose — but if I do, the evidence will point right at you, Autumn."

"Do you think I tried to kill you, Max?" Autumn asked gently.

"No, I don't," Max said emphatically. "But it will sure look like it to the police."

"I don't think you did it either, Mother," Roycie said abruptly.

Autumn leaned over and hugged him to her, saying with a tremor in her voice, "Thank you, Roycie. I really didn't do it, whatever it looks like."

She looked up at Max. "And I'm beginning to think that I didn't kill my husband, either. This is a definite frame job, so why couldn't the other have been?"

"I'm thinking farther, yet," Max said. "You said your father and your doctor boyfriend had everything to live for. What if they were both murdered, too?"

A shudder swept over Autumn's body. Her voice shrank almost to a whisper. "Max, this is terrifying! Could someone in my family really be a murderer, maybe even a multiple one? And have planned to make me look like the killer?"

She shook her head in disbelief. "It's preposterous!"

"I agree, but we have to consider the facts."

"What are we going to do?" Autumn asked. She looked around and lowered her voice. "Who could be doing this? I'm really scared — and I don't know who I can trust."

"Do you think your brother is capable of murder?"

"I don't know," Autumn said. "It is difficult to think any of my family could be a killer."

"Maybe we had better discuss this another time," Max said, glancing down. They had forgotten Roycie, who was taking in everything that was said with round, frightened eyes.

"I think you're right," Autumn agreed, quickly catching his meaning.

"What's going on here?" a voice asked from behind them.

Startled, they all three turned and saw Autumn's mother standing in the doorway of the *corredore*, leaning on her black cane.

"Mother," Autumn walked toward her, "someone just tried to kill Max. Someone from our house!"

Shock registered on Cecilia's aristocratic face and she said quickly, "Autumn, don't be ridiculous! What possible reason could anyone have here for killing the neighbor's chauffeur?"

"Roycie saw someone push a big clay pot off on Max," Autumn said. "If he hadn't called out a warning, Max would have been killed."

Cecilia's eyes widened. She turned to Roycie and spoke sharply, "You saw who did this thing? Who was it?"

Roycie hesitated and his grandmother moved toward him, saying gently, "Don't be afraid, dear. Who did you see?"

"Yes, Roycie, go ahead and tell who you saw," said the mocking voice of Sherman from behind them.

Roycie jumped visibly and then said faintly, "It was someone in a-a blue dress with red hair." But he raised his voice and said defiantly, "But it wasn't M-Mother! I know it wasn't!"

"Wasn't it?" Sherman said derisively. "Didn't you just now say it was a redhead wearing a blue dress?"

He waved his arm dramatically. "No one here is wearing a blue dress except your mother, and no one else is redheaded," he paused, and then finished with a smirk on his unpleasant face, "except our eavesdropping sister just inside yon door." He chuckled maliciously.

Audra stepped into the room, her plain

face red with embarrassment. She raised her chin contemptuously and shot a malevolent look at her brother. "Yes, I was eavesdropping. What of it? I just wanted to know what was going on!"

"Don't worry, you aren't guilty of trying to murder our chauffeur friend here. Your hair is a *dull* shade of red, and you certainly are not wearing a blue dress."

"Sherman!" Cecilia spoke sharply, "behave yourself!"

"Well, our dear sister says one of us is an attempted murderer! I was just pointing out that she is the only one who fits the description by the only eyewitness!"

"I'm sure none of us did such a terrible thing!" Cecilia said sharply.

Autumn's face was very pale, but she had said nothing during Sherman's baiting. Now her eyes swept over the occupants of the room as she spoke in a low but calm voice, "Someone in this house attempted to kill Max a while ago. And whoever did it, wore the dress I had laid out to wear today, to make it look like I did it!"

Audra spoke angrily, "Autumn, you are accusing your own flesh and blood! And your son said the person wearing the blue dress had red hair." She sent a withering glance Sherman's way before she said testily, "My hair was never red like yours. Even before it began to turn grey, it was auburn!"

"I'm not saying you did it, Audra. I'm saying someone in this house tried to kill him."

"What about the doctor?"

Everyone turned to look at Max when he spoke for the first time.

Cecilia spoke stiffly. "That is as absurd as the intimation that our immediate family members committed this heinous act. Why would he want to kill you?"

"I don't know, but perhaps I should turn this whole thing over to the police and let them get to the bottom of it."

"I wouldn't do that if I were you," a new voice spoke at the edge of the circle. No one had seen Dr. Marler come out onto the *corredore*.

"Why not?" Max challenged.

"This family has suffered enough already through the unpleasantness of one accident, two suicides, and one murder. I'm sure the Mexican police would like nothing better than to get their hands on an American and be able to prove murder. Don't you think our little Autumn has been through enough without being incarcerated in a Mexican prison?"

Cecilia gasped. "Don't say such a thing,

Laurence! Autumn did not try to murder Max."

"I don't think she did either, but the police will. The description of the murderer fits only her in this household."

He turned his slight body toward Autumn. "By the way, what makes you think someone from this household did it?"

"Because whoever did it was wearing my dress!" Autumn said.

"Then how do you happen to be wearing it?"

"I was taking a bath and when I came out it was back in my room. All except the belt! We found it lying on the stairs going down into my *sala*. The killer was probably in a hurry to get the dress back in my room before I got out of my bath and missed it!"

Bright spots of color had appeared in Autumn's face and her eyes flashed. "And I'm also beginning to wonder if I killed my husband. That was just too pat! Just like this is!"

Sherman raised his eyebrows in mock horror. "My, we are getting beside ourselves! The courts convicted you, sister dear!"

"And you all didn't help me a bit," Autumn lashed out angrily. "You were the ones who *really* convicted me!"

Cecilia moved laboriously across the room using her cane, and laid a delicate hand on her daughter's arm. "Autumn," she said soothingly, "I think you had better go to your room, dear. You are saying things that you don't really mean."

Her grey eyes — so like Autumn's — were gentle but firm. "We all did what we could, even to getting you out of the hospital as soon as possible. You know that. We may not be a demonstrative family, but we stand behind our own.

"Now be a good girl and go to bed for awhile. This little incident has upset you. Perhaps Dr. Marler will give you something to make you sleep for awhile."

"No! I don't want a sedative, and I am not going to bed!" Autumn said sharply.

"Very well," her mother said in an offended tone. "I was just trying to help."

"Max, what are your plans?" Sherman said with a half-grin. "Are you calling in the coppers?"

"I'll wait until the Windthorns come in today, and see what they say."

"That sounds like a good plan," agreed the doctor.

He walked over to Autumn. "Young lady, I think you should at least go down and have some nourishment. I don't like your color."

His voice was kind. "And believe me, child, none of us have ever had anything but your interests at heart. I think you know that when you aren't all wrought up."

Abruptly, he turned to Max. "I can hardly accept your story that someone deliberately pushed a clay pot off on you. Things do fall accidentally, you know."

"I saw someone push it off on Max," Roycie spoke up.

"You saw someone push it off?"

"Well, I never really saw the person push it off, but I saw her after it fell."

"Did you get a good look?" the doctor persisted.

"Yes! The person crawled real quick but I saw her."

"Children have big imaginations," Dr. Marler said. "Maybe the morning sun was in your eyes, and you just thought you saw a person."

"No, I saw a person in a blue dress."

"Maybe one of the maids knocked it off accidentally and then ran away because she was afraid she would be accused of doing it deliberately."

"But the person had red hair and wore a blue dress."

"Juana, the housemaid, has a red cast to her hair. In the morning sun, it would have looked red. And anyone could have been wearing a blue Mexican dress. The maids often wear such dresses to work in because they are so loose and comfortable.

"It could have been Juana, couldn't it, Roycie? After all, no one would have a reason to hurt your friend."

"I-I guess." Roycie looked at Max. "Maybe it was Juana. Maybe no one meant to hurt you." His voice was hopeful.

Autumn looked at Roycie and said sharply, "Do you really think it was Juana?"

"I-I don't know," Roycie said. "I-I'm all mixed up now. But maybe it was."

"I'll be going," Max said. "I've got work to do." And he did, but he also wanted to get away and think this thing through. In his heart, he was confident Roycie's first story was the true one, but it was just as well for the child to believe otherwise for now.

"I'll walk down with you," Autumn said. "Roycie, I think you should go with Aunt Audra to have some breakfast."

They were both silent until they reached the gate. Then Autumn spoke, "What do you think, Max? You don't really believe it was an accident, do you?"

"Not really," Max said. "What about the crowbar we found?"

"And the belt to my dress on the stairs,"

Autumn supplied. "Please be careful, Max."

"I plan to," he said grimly. "I have to go in and do some things before the Windthorns come, but I think you should be very careful, too, Autumn. You made some accusations that could put you in danger, if they are true."

Autumn's face was pale but determined, "I know. But I don't really think anyone would harm me as long as you are around. They would know you would call in the police for an investigation."

She swallowed hard. "Max, this is so frightening. It is almost a certainty now that someone in my house wants to harm me — and I don't know who!"

22

Skye and Joy came home a little past noon. Both were tired, but Skye said the trip had been very beneficial to the work he was doing on some ancient writing.

"We called my dad," Joy said. "Mitzie and Terry are both doing fine and looking forward to school being out in two weeks. Then they are all coming down here. I can hardly wait. I've missed those kids so much!"

"I've missed them a lot, too," Skye said. "But we knew they would be in good hands. I'm glad your folks could come and help Washington with the children."

As soon as he could, Max gave Skye and Joy a full account of his being drugged again and of Dr. Otero's report that the drug was mescaline. He told them briefly about the three days of sightseeing with Autumn and Roycie and ended with the attempt on his life that morning.

Skye whistled. "Wow! I think we had better stay around and take care of you! You lead a hazardous life!" Then he sobered and said gravely, "Seriously, what do you make of this? Do you really think Roycie saw someone after that pot fell?"

"He was too shaken *not* to have seen someone. At first he just knew the person was Autumn."

"Do you think it might have been?"

"I'm positive it wasn't," Max said. "She said she didn't do it, and I believe her. I'd stake my life on it."

"But why would anyone want to kill you, Max?" Joy asked.

"I don't know, but it must have something to do with Autumn." He told them about their confrontation with Autumn's family members and Dr. Marler. "Should we call the police?"

But the Windthorns were reluctant to involve the Mexican police in the situation.

"The Mexican courts would probably send Autumn to prison since all the evidence points to her," Skye said. "I'm with you. I don't really believe she tried to kill you."

Autumn called that evening and said all was calm there.

"I'm glad you called. I was just about to call you," Max said. "Pastor Hernandez called to invite you and Roycie to church tomorrow and also for Sunday dinner. I have eaten there before; you can expect a treat."

Delighted, Autumn said they would be ready.

"Max, how handsome you look!" Autumn exclaimed when he appeared the next morning to take them to church.

"Oh, sure," Max scoffed. "With this ugly mug of mine, it's a wonder I don't scare all the kids away from Sunday School."

Autumn's smile vanished and she said gently, "Max, you sell yourself short. Your face mirrors gentleness, integrity, strength — and Jesus Christ. It's a face with character. Don't ever apologize for it."

"And your suit is pretty, too," Roycie said.

"Thanks," Max mumbled. Unaccustomed to compliments on his appearance, he felt his face getting red, though he was vastly pleased. He had dressed carefully for this occasion. His tawny head and freshly clipped, short beard glistened in the morning sun, setting off his dark cream suit and tie with contrasting blue silk shirt. His black shoes were shined to a mirror finish.

Max was proud of his friends when he escorted them into church a short while later. Autumn was beautiful in a simple white dress and hat while Roycie looked scrubbed and handsome in a tan silk Mexican shirt and brown corded pants.

Autumn was amazed when Skye played the piano for the service; she recognized his very obvious talent. Later, he accompanied Joy who sang a song in Spanish. Her voice was not trained, but it had a moving quality that was very stirring.

Since neither Eduardo nor his wife spoke English, during the meal that followed the service all the conversation was in Spanish. If anyone ran into difficulty, Skye translated for them. He was surprisingly proficient in the language.

When Joy mentioned that Autumn was a singer, the pastor quickly asked if she would sing for them the next Sunday.

"I don't know any Christian songs," Autumn demurred. "In fact, I only know two songs in Spanish, and they aren't appropriate for church," she said with a smile.

"If you feel like practicing, I'll help you learn one this next week," Joy said persuasively. "Skye could accompany you on the piano."

"That would be fun," Autumn agreed with alacrity.

After dinner, they all climbed into the Windthorn station wagon for the trip home. Max, at the wheel, steered the vehicle out into the line of traffic. Suddenly, through the rearview mirror he saw a rusty grey Volkswagen van pull into the lane of traffic two cars behind the Windthorn station wagon. They were being followed again!

Anger lanced through Max. If he had been alone, he would have tried to find out who the person was and what he wanted. But not wishing to upset Autumn and Roycie, who had been through enough lately, he kept still, but his eyes kept glancing at the image in the rearview mirror.

On the trip home, Autumn sat in front with Max, but Skye invited Roycie to sit in back with him and Joy. The child was all eyes, bouncing up and down, trying to see everything at once. Skye pointed out different places of interest, adding little bits of information about the ones he knew.

"Didn't Dorotea fix a delicious meal?" Autumn exclaimed to Max. "She was so sweet, too. You know, I have never really gotten acquainted with the Mexican people," she confessed. "I didn't know they were such delightful, dear people. I see why you want to work here, Max. I'm already looking forward to seeing the Hernandezes next Sunday."

"We love them, too," Joy said from the back seat. "The service today didn't tire you too much?"

247

"No. I'm getting stronger every day so that I can really enjoy things again," Autumn said. "I'm thinking of going to another doctor for a check-up. Dr. Marler insisted on having a doctor friend of his examine me when he suspected I had cancer and that physician confirmed Dr. Marler's diagnosis. Do you suppose both doctors could have been wrong?"

"Did you know the other doctor who examined you?" Max asked.

"No, he was a colleague of Dr. Marler's." Her eyes widened and she exclaimed, "You aren't suggesting that — that. . . ."

"It would probably not be wise to question your doctor's diagnosis until you have had another doctor examine you," Skye interrupted. "Why not go to Dr. Otero? He's a reputable doctor whom I know well. He's absolutely reliable."

"I'll call him for an appointment tomorrow," Autumn said. Her voice faltered, and she clasped her hands together tightly. "If only Dr. Marler is wrong, and I'm not going to die!"

23

Autumn called Max a short while after Max took them home. She sounded distraught. "Max, I had planned to see Dr. Otero on the sly because I knew what a fuss the family would make if I didn't.

"Roycie was so interested in the things he was seeing that I never dreamed he paid any attention to what was said in the car. But we had hardly gotten home when he informed the whole family that I was going to have Dr. Otero examine me because I thought Dr. Marler was wrong about my illness!"

"Were they awfully upset?"

"Upset is far too mild a word to use! They happened to all be together in the main *sala* watching TV — even Dr. Marler.

"We barely got in the room when Roycie dropped his bombshell. Dr. Marler looked like I had slapped him in the face; mother and Audra acted as if I had committed the unpardonable sin. Sherman, of course, made the sarcastic remark, 'So you think our doctor cousin is a quack?' "

"But it shouldn't be a crime to go to another doctor to verify a diagnosis as serious as cancer, or even to get a check-up," Max protested.

Autumn drew in her breath sharply. "You don't know my family! Mother looked at me like I was a traitor. You see, our family has used Laurence for as long as I can remember — loyalty to family and all. Mother has always been a matriarch in our home, and she holds his ability in high regard. She considers this an insult to her judgment, too."

"I'm not sure what a matriarch is," Max said, "but I think I get the drift. Are you still going to see Dr. Otero?"

"Yes! I tried to appease Mother and Laurence by telling them I hadn't meant to make them feel badly, but I thought another doctor's opinion wouldn't hurt since I had been feeling so well lately."

"How did they take that?"

"Laurence still acted huffy, but he grudgingly said if it would make me feel better to go ahead."

"And your mother and the rest?"

"Sherman didn't act like it mattered to him either way, but Audra looked daggers at me and told me I should be ashamed of myself. She said, 'I suppose that chauffeur friend next door influenced you to do this, and you would naturally take his advice before that of your own flesh and blood.' "

"Perhaps we have influenced you," Max said. "I'm sorry if it's caused a rift in your family."

"Don't worry about it," Autumn said. "Mother calmed down pretty soon. She took it better than I would have imagined. She's always the peacemaker of the family. She chided Audra for being so catty and told her if getting another doctor's opinion would set my mind at ease, then she'd go along with it."

"Good," said Max. "I'll take you to see the doctor if you want me to."

"Thanks so much," Autumn said gratefully. "I appreciate that. If you'll give me Dr. Otero's number, I'll call first thing in the morning and get an appointment. I hope I can get in this week. I'm anxious to hear his verdict."

"Just don't get your hopes up about that verdict," Max cautioned.

"I'm trying not to," Autumn said as she hung up.

Max had trouble going to sleep that night. He had warned Autumn not to get her hopes too high and found he had not taken his own advice. He kept thinking of the future as if Autumn were an established part of it.

251

He finally managed to get to sleep after he had given himself a stern lecture. "You could be attending Autumn's funeral in a few months, Max," he reminded himself brutally — out loud.

"And even if Autumn were to live, she'd go back to her career and forget all about you. Or, at least, she could never be more to you than a friend.

"If you ever had any brains, Max Parrish, you lost 'em when you let yourself dream about Autumn Caldwell. Can you seriously imagine that peaches and cream complexion, those soft, manicured hands out in the sun and dirt of a backwoods Mexican village? Beautiful Autumn washing clothes on a scrub board, living in a house with no running water and no bathroom? Bathing in a muddy stream? Fighting bugs and mosquitoes for a night's sleep?"

Max chuckled grimly. His imagination was good, especially where Autumn was concerned, and the whole picture he had painted was laughable and ridiculous. Unthinkable!

"I wouldn't want a life like that for her," he muttered. It was his last conscious thought as he drifted into sleep.

It was hours later when something woke him. The first sounds only lightly penetrated his sleep. Then, suddenly, they pierced his consciousness and he snapped wide awake. He sat up in bed, his ears alert for the noise that had awakened him; his eyes searched the room for any movement.

He waited with rapidly beating heart and bated breath. His pulse quickened as he strove to hear. He had the unnerving feeling that whatever had awakened him was poised, and listening, also.

Then he heard a slight rustle and — more a sensation than a sound — a faint footstep. It seemed to come from the bathroom.

Max eased out of bed. His bedroom was almost totally dark so he moved with slow deliberate steps so he wouldn't trip over anything.

Reaching the corner of the bathroom which projected out into the room, Max eased along the wall. The bathroom door was just a few feet beyond the corner.

The bathroom door opened into the bedroom, and he always left it open. Reaching the door jamb, he steadied himself with his right hand, and reached for the light switch with his left. But his hand encountered a solid surface.

The door was closed!

His left hand groped for and closed upon the doorknob. He tried to turn it. It was locked! From the inside!

His heart pounding, Max stood for a moment trying to decide what to do. He heard another slight sound and then a scrape and click as if someone was moving his toilet articles about on the shelf inside. Max cocked his head and listened intently. Why would a prowler be in his bathroom?

Max made a sudden decision. Moving back out of line with the door, in case the intruder had a gun, Max called out. "Come out of there! I know you're in there, and there's no chance you can get away. Come on out before I break the door down!"

For a moment there was complete silence. Then Max heard hushed footsteps, followed by a sliding sound. He thought he heard faint footfalls again briefly, but he wasn't sure, then all was quiet.

Max could hear his own breathing in the absolute silence. "Come on out!" Max ordered again, "or I'm going to knock the door down!"

Standing very still, Max felt quivers run down his back. Had the person fled? If so, how did he get out of the bathroom? There was no other door.

Max waited for several long moments. Then he eased over and shook the doorknob. "Come on out, I say, or I'll. . . ."

He broke off in astonishment. The door wasn't locked! Turning the handle quickly, Max pushed back the door and jumped away from the opening, fearing a trap.

But after he had waited a couple of minutes and not a sound reached his ears, Max reached across soundlessly and flipped on the light.

Everything was as still as death. Max peered into the room. There was no one there. Cautiously, he slid into the room and stared about. It was empty!

Puzzled, Max stood in the middle of the bathroom and pondered. Had the sounds come from somewhere else? He went swiftly to the other rooms and turned on the lights. There was no one in his suite, and the doors were all still securely locked.

Returning to his bathroom, Max tried to recall the sounds. Clicking bottles, a sliding sound, and faint footsteps. The sounds had not been loud but they had been very real. He felt the hair on the back of his neck stand up.

"Now, Max," he reasoned with himself aloud, "this isn't a ghost who keeps coming into your room. It's a real, blood and bones person. And a real person has to have a door or an opening of some kind to come through.

"Hmmm," Max said. He rose and walked to the cabinet where he kept his toiletries and opened the door. "I heard these bottles rattle together. What was someone after?"

Then a thought surfaced that caused fear in his throat. Was the intruder poisoning his toiletries now?

His shaving lotion and deodorant were laying on their sides. He had used them both that morning, so someone had definitely been in his cabinet. But why? And how?

There has to be a hidden door or panel in this room, he decided. Otherwise, the person could not have gotten away.

He searched the whole room — even to stepping down into his sunken bathtub and sliding his hands over each tile. He twisted the smooth, green, ceramic frog, whose open mouth held his bath soap. He ran his hand around the gold, built-in tiled planter at the head of his tub that held green ivy, but he found no hidden openings or switches. Completely baffled, Max stepped out of the bathtub and stood in the middle of the room to think.

The overturned bottles in his cabinet seemed to be the only things disturbed. He stepped over to it and took everything out to be sure there was no catch or switch behind them. Yet, there must be a hidden opening in this room and a switch or catch to open it!

Suddenly his eyes narrowed as he looked calculatingly at the toiletry cabinet. Taking hold of one side of the cabinet, he tugged gingerly. Nothing happened. He moved to the other side and tugged. Without warning, the cabinet swung out with a sliding sound. Behind it was a small, black doorway. Max stuck his head in and saw a very narrow stairway descending into the darkness.

Heart pounding, Max hurried to his bedroom and brought back a powerful flashlight. Shining it into the narrow corridor, he saw the treads leading to a small landing, a dozen feet below.

Max ran back into his bedroom and hastily dressed. Returning to the bathroom, he climbed into the narrow opening. It was a tight squeeze for someone his size. Flashing the light ahead, he moved down the steps. He was thankful for his soft, crepe rubber shoe soles; they made no sound.

At the landing, the stairs took a sharp right turn. Directing the flashlight beam down the stone steps, he could just see a heavy wooden door at the foot of the stairs. Descending silently, Max reached the door and lifted the heavy latch. To his surprise, the door swung out on quiet, well-oiled hinges.

Max switched his light off and stepped into the doorway.

24

Max stood for a few minutes in the total darkness, listening. Finally, he turned on his light. Sweeping it around, he saw he was in a large room. A swaybacked couch, a few dilapidated chairs, and an ancient, paint-peeled table were the only furnishings. Dust and cobwebs covered everything.

Max turned the light on the floor. A trail of footprints in the heavy dust led across the room to a far door. He knelt down and studied them. There were no clear prints, so he played the light once more about the room. The only door out of this room — besides the small one behind him — seemed to be the one to which the shoe prints led.

Max crossed the room quickly, his soft-soled shoes whispering in the dust. When he reached the doorway, he switched off the light and listened intently, but he could hear no sound beyond the door.

Taking a deep breath, he put his hand on the doorknob and turned it. Somewhat surprised when the door moved, he pushed it open slightly, and peered around it.

Beyond, a single bare lightbulb hung from the ceiling, illuminating a wide corridor.

Stepping into the hallway, Max glanced at the floor. Although not spotless, no dust had accumulated there. Directly across the hall was another door. Max walked to it and gingerly tried the handle.

The door swung open silently to reveal a large room similar to the dust-covered one he had just come through. Only this room was clean of dust — and was completely empty. His flashlight revealed two other doors in the room, a large one at the end of the room to his right, and a small door directly across from where he stood.

Max sprinted softly down the length of the room to try the door on the right. It was locked. Moving quickly to the small door, he tried that handle. The door opened easily.

Glancing inside, he saw a narrow stairway leading upward, identical to the one under his bathroom. Max eased the door closed. Without a doubt it led up into Autumn's house.

Feeling like a trespasser, Max quickly retraced his steps through the large room and into the corridor. Closing the door softly on the big room, Max leaned against it, uncertain what he should do now.

This part of the basement was being used by someone in Autumn's house. Although he felt like he was trespassing on private quarters, he was certain that the person who had drugged him had come through here to do so.

Well, since I've come this far, I'll try to find out what is going on down here, he decided.

It all fit together. Autumn had said she had heard hushed footsteps and strange voices below her room and thought there might be a basement under the big house. Something clandestine *was* taking place within her house.

A little bell of warning began to ring in his mind: someone had tried to kill him the day before. That someone could very well be here in the darkness, lying in wait for him.

Max returned to the large dust-laden room and searched until he found a heavy wooden chair leg. He hoped it would not be necessary, but he didn't want to be completely defenseless.

Letting himself into the dimly lighted corridor again, Max saw two more doors on each side of the hallway. He looked into the two on his right first, flashing his light around. Both were dirty and littered with broken, discarded furniture and a few boxes of old magazines and rags.

Max checked the corridor before crossing the hall. There was no sign of anyone else's presence but his own. Striding across the corridor, he opened the last door on that side.

Pay dirt! This room was spacious and softly lighted. His eyes widened with surprise at its contents. Soft carpeting covered the floor; luxurious couches and inviting plush chairs were scattered about. Tasteful pictures decorated the soft, cream colored walls. Varnished beams in the ceiling lent a warm, cozy atmosphere. Polished walnut tables and a large-screen TV completed the furnishings.

Max walked quickly to an open door on his left and looked in. This room was also richly carpeted but the right-hand wall was sectioned into small cubicles with closed doors. He crossed to the first one; opening the door, he looked inside.

It contained a comfortable-looking couch, a matching reclining chair, and a small polished table with a lamp.

Mystified, Max checked the next small room, and it was also furnished in exactly the same simple luxury.

Everything was spotlessly clean. Turning around, Max examined the larger portion of the room. Near a door that he realized was the other door off the corridor, stood a double metal file cabinet. Nearby was an upholstered office chair and a huge walnut desk. Its polished surface was partly covered by a large green blotter. Pens and a few other desk accessories were neatly tucked into a marble holder.

Max walked to the hall door and started to go out. Then he turned back. Something about these rooms teased his memory, but it kept edging away when he tried to focus on it.

He drew in his breath and slowly exhaled as he studied the room. Then suddenly it struck him like a blow from the club he still carried in his hand.

The odor in the room! It was faint but distinct. The scent was harsh and sweet, like burning rope or dried grasses. Marijuana! His heart seemed to leap into his throat. Was this a secret meeting place for illegal drug buys? Was someone in Autumn's house a drug dealer?

A cold wind seemed to chill Max to the marrow of his bones. His association with drug dealers when his mother was alive had been fraught with danger and terror. He knew the unsavory, evil men and women who seemed to have no conscience and showed no mercy to anyone who got in their way!

A feeling of extreme urgency settled upon him. His only desire now was to get back — and quickly — to the safety of his own apartment.

Max took one last quick look about the room and started for the hall door. But before he reached it, it swung open noiselessly. Max stopped dead in his tracks. Standing shoulder to shoulder in the doorway were two of the biggest pit bulls he had ever seen.

They made no threatening sound or movement, but their watchful, alert silence was doubly menacing as they stood barring his way. Beneath short, glossy coats, their stocky, well-muscled bodies were powerfully built. The solid reddish-tan one, Max thought was a male. It was slightly bigger than the predominantly white and brindle one he took as the female. Both had formidable wedge-like muzzles, powerful jaws, and blocky heads.

Max glimpsed a jagged scar on the male's throat and another on his shimmering red-tan shoulder. He knew this pit bull had probably known the dog-fighting pit intimately. Since it was alive, he also knew it had killed.

Both dogs stared at him impassively for a moment, then the big male started forward, slowly and deliberately, his eyes intent on Max. The female, about a shoulder's length behind, paced beside him. Neither made a sound.

Slowly Max began to inch his way back — back toward one of the small rooms. If he could reach the door, he might stand a better chance of survival. His hand gripped the chair leg club, and he silently breathed a prayer for help.

A cold sweat broke out upon Max's body as the pit bulls advanced. He knew the viciousness of some of this breed of dog. Even small pit bulls could maim and kill, their powerful jaws attacking repeatedly, tearing and ripping like a shark. And he judged these two as large ones, probably over a hundred pounds each.

Praying desperately, Max strove to calm his fears. He knew how fear could stupefy the brain and petrify one's limbs. A clear, alert mind was his best weapon right now.

Suddenly, he knew he wasn't going to make it to the door! The bigger pit bull was bunching his muscles, preparing to leap, his eyes steady upon Max's throat. Max gripped the club and prepared to swing. Perhaps with the heavy flashlight in his left hand, he could deflect the attack of the female briefly while he tried to deal a hopefully stunning blow to the head of the male. His muscles tensed for the attack.

His eyes were so intent on the animals that when the command blared out, he started, almost dropping the club.

"Stop!"

Both animals stopped instantly, poised as if for a picture.

Sherman stepped inside the doorway. His eyes were hot with anger. Gone was his indolent, mocking indifference.

Easing in between the dogs, he laid a long-fingered hand upon each head, but he kept his blazing eyes upon Max.

"You stupid, blundering fool!" he hissed.

"I've been called such before," Max said dryly.

"Why didn't you stay out of my affairs? I can't let you go back and blab all you know to the whole world! How'd you find this place, anyway?"

"I heard a noise in my bathroom and checked it out. I found the stairs and knew whoever had come into my locked apartment and drugged me had come in that way. I meant to find out who did it. And I guess I did."

For the first time, Sherman relaxed his angry, tense stance slightly. His laugh rang out, a bitter, mocking sound without real mirth. His two dogs looked up at him quizzically.

"Yeah! That was me. I doped your juice, and then danced and played the flute for you. Pretty good acting, huh? I'll bet you thought it was the beautiful Autumn, didn't you?

"But I thought Autumn's black rose on your pillow and the black widow spiders in your bed was a touch of real genius, if I do say so."

"Not for long. Her denial had the ring of truth," Max said dryly.

If I can only gain some time, maybe I can get out of this alive yet, Max thought. He had left the cabinet pulled out to reveal the stairway in his bathroom. It shouldn't be long until daylight. If Skye or a maid found the opening, they would know where he was. He had to keep Sherman talking! It was his only chance. *Dear Father, help me now!*

He tried to be calm. "Your act was pretty convincing. I suppose the red hair was a wig."

"Borrowed from my dear sister's own boudoir," Sherman bantered; then his eyes grew hostile and bitter. "I'm sure *she* couldn't explain the flute playing, but I can play as well as she does, if anyone had ever thought to notice! Dear papa — rest his poor blind soul — never knew he had a son! His whole life was tied up in Autumn, and no one else existed! Well, he got what he had coming!"

"*You* killed him?"

Sherman stared at Max incredulously. "Me? No, I didn't! But I never grieved for him." His eyes grew sly, and he lowered his voice mysteriously. "I've always suspected Autumn did him in."

"I don't believe it!"

"You — nor any other man she bewitched, including my father — would ever believe she could do any wrong! But doesn't the four men she was closest to dying under strange circumstances mean anything to you, you stupid fool!"

Max could feel goosebumps on his arms. Sherman was convinced his sister had murdered those men! *Could I have been duped by one of the best actresses in the business?*

"Wise up, man!" Sherman said derisively. "That woman tried to kill *you* yesterday. I found the crowbar she used to push that heavy clay planter off with!"

"She couldn't have," Max protested, but his denial sounded weak even in his own ears. "How do I know you didn't try to kill me?"

"Just my word," Sherman said. "But I

swear to you, I never lifted a hand to kill you.

"I meant to scare you off from my sister with the drugging. After all, Sis is going to die soon. You might have got her to the altar and why should any of her money go to a new husband? It costs a lot to live these days, and I want as large a slice of her pie as I can wrangle!"

"Did you kill her husband so you could get his part?" Max asked.

Sherman's eyes narrowed, "You're sure full of questions! But no, I did not! I never killed a person in my life."

"Then why start now?" Max said. "Dealing drugs wouldn't bring anything like a sentence for murder."

"If I let you go, you'd tell everything, and even if I managed to escape a jail sentence, my sweet money-making deal here would be finished. I get a lot of money for this racket."

"Dealing drugs is a dirty way to make money," Max said. "Is it worth ruining and wrecking lives?"

"They'd get it somewhere," Sherman said. "Can I help it if people are stupid enough to sell their souls for drugs? Besides, I don't actually sell any drugs. My part of the deal is to furnish a luxurious place for rich businessmen to get high. The dealers brought in the furnishings; their janitor keeps it clean."

Sherman grinned conspiratorially. "These operators deal with high rollers — wealthy businessmen from other countries, especially Japan. They don't bring them here all the time. There are other hideaway places set up here and there around the city. That way no one place becomes conspicuous by having too many visitors, too often."

"And they usually come late at night," Max added. "Autumn said she sometimes heard strange voices and footsteps in the night. But everyone laughed at her and said she was imagining things."

"Yeah, it's unfortunate that the outside entrance leads through a hallway under her rooms. I've tried to get my 'guests' to be quieter since then, but sometimes they forget. However, our family doesn't take Autumn seriously. She's sick, and sometimes has nightmares, so her words are no threat to my business.

"If things got sticky, we'd just shut this place down till it was no longer under suspicion. They've even had a spy on your trail night and day since you got involved with my sister. If you were an undercover cop, they meant to knock you off or buy you off."

"The Mexican with the little gold ring in his ear?"

Sherman's grin was nasty. "He's a hit man when they need one, too. A pleasant young man! This is a big operation — and smart. They even have spies in the police department so they know what's going on. They'd be hard to catch, believe me!"

"Don't be too sure," Max said. "There're some honest people left. Someone will catch 'em after a while."

"Don't hold your breath till it happens," Sherman scoffed. He moved back and leaned indolently on the doorframe.

"I hate to do this to you, Max, honestly I do. I don't relish blood and violence. I'm going to have to leave you now. But you won't be lonely; Satan and Sarah are going to stay with you, for a bit anyway."

At the names, the two big dogs looked up at him. The female licked his hand and laid her head against his leg affectionately. The male thrust his head into one of his hands to have it scratched.

A warm light came in Sherman's eyes as he patted the two big dogs. "I used to go to dogfights," he said. "Satan here was the meanest fighter on four legs, and he made lots of money for his master. But he finally met his match. A black monster of a pit bull broke both his front legs and tore his throat up so bad he looked like a goner.

"They left him lying in the ring bleeding to death. The ring was way out in the country, but when everyone left, I got him to a vet quick. Satan survived, and he seemed to know I saved his life. He's as gentle as a baby with me . . . but he hates everyone else.

"I searched around until I found a female pup with huge parents. I plan to raise their pups to sell as fighting dogs."

"That's a cruel future for any dog!"

Sherman laughed. "Don't you believe it! When they're bred for it, a pit bull lives to fight."

"What does Autumn think of your plans to sell dogs for the fighting pits?"

"She doesn't know I have the dogs down here. None of my family does — or even knows there's a basement. It's none of their business! I keep them in a locked room when the drug parties are going on. Then, I let my 'lovelies' loose to guard the basement at night. I wouldn't like to see what a person looked like who tried to invade my party-house down here."

He turned away with a grin. "That's what happened to one Max Parrish, a chauffeur of the Windthorns and admirer of the fair Autumn. The one-time jewel thief went back to a life of crime. He broke into the basement of wealthy Autumn Caldwell, intent on making off with her jewels."

Sherman's chuckle was sadistic. "But the family guard dogs surprised him in the act and when he was found, his mutilated body was torn so badly the casket could not be opened for viewing."

Max felt his heart pumping fiercely and his hands felt damp and hot. "You can't do this, Sherman! It's murder!"

Sherman turned a contemptuous sneer on Max. "Can't I? Just watch me."

A stern voice spoke from the doorway, "No, you can't do that, Sherman! I won't allow it!"

In the doorway stood Cecilia, Sherman's diminutive mother, dressed in a rose-colored robe and leaning on her black cane.

25

Sherman's skin paled, and his face went tense with surprise and something close to fear.

Then he seemed to take hold of himself. Drawing himself up, he spoke in a firm voice, "Mother, this is not your affair. Please go back upstairs. This man broke into our house — probably to steal us blind, and if I let the dogs rough him up a little, it is only what he deserves."

His mother stood regally, resting part of her weight on the black cane. Her blue-grey eyes calmly regarded Sherman for a moment, then she said gently, "It's no use trying to deceive me, Son, I've been standing here long enough to hear all about this business of yours."

She snapped her fingers at the dogs and both came to her happily, rubbing their heads against her and looking up adoringly.

Sherman batted his eyes and gasped, "Th-they act like they know you."

Cecilia laughed softly. "All dogs like me, Sherman. They know I like them."

"I-it's unbelievable," Sherman said incredulously.

"Not really," his mother said. She stroked the dogs' heads and then straightened up and said severely, "Sherman, I cannot express how deeply distressed I am that you would open our home to drug traffickers. If you had been caught, we would all have ended up in a Mexican prison!"

Sherman tried to speak, but she silenced him with a queenly motion of her small, shapely hand.

"Now, I'll tell you what we are going to do. You will inform your drug people that you're afraid your family is getting suspicious and that they can no longer use our house for their operation."

"I can't do that!"

She fixed her eyes upon him and said with asperity, "You can and you will! Otherwise I will go to the police with this!"

"You wouldn't!"

"I would and you know I would!"

Sherman looked thoroughly shaken, his eyes miserable, as he looked into his mother's unflinching gaze. Suddenly, his shoulders slumped. "Okay, if I must."

He suddenly seemed to remember Max. "And what about him?" he asked, jerking his thumb toward him. "He'll blab to the cops for sure if we let him go."

"I've been thinking about that," Cecilia said. She turned speculative eyes upon Max. "Max, in return for rescuing you from a certain and horrible death, I'm requiring a favor of you."

"Yes, ma'am?"

"If Sherman agrees to end this drug operation, I want your promise that you will not report what went on down here to the police. I think he has learned his lesson. Is it a deal?"

Max hesitated. Since he had become a Christian, he had been extremely careful to obey the law, scrupulously so.

Cecilia's eyes grew shrewd. "Would it make you feel righteous if Autumn, myself, and Audra ended up with Sherman in a Mexican prison? After all, we had no part in this, but I'm sure the police will not believe that.

"Besides, I understand you once were involved with unlawful activities. Someone gave you a chance to straighten up your life. Won't you extend the same chance to my son?"

"Okay," Max decided. "If Sherman is willing to give up this business for good."

"Sherman?" Cecilia asked, turning her gentle face toward her son. "Do you agree

276

to terminate this drug business once and for all?"

"All right," he said reluctantly.

Cecilia stepped over and patted Sherman's face with a soft hand. "Good boy! You'll thank us when you give this some real consideration. Sooner or later you would likely have been killed by some of these men. I'm sure drug dealers are not to be trusted."

She stopped to stroke the dogs one more time. "Now," Cecilia said, straightening her back and shifting the black cane on the floor. "Max and I are going. Please call your pets and keep them in this room until we are gone. I'm not sure they would obey my commands as well as they do yours."

Sherman spoke a sharp, "Come!" and both dogs obediently moved to his side. As Max edged gingerly around them to the door, Satan moved uneasily but Sherman settled him down with a sharp, "Stay!"

Trying to not move too quickly, Max eased out the door.

Cecilia closed the door firmly on the watchful dogs and a sullen Sherman.

"Come with me quickly," Cecilia whispered urgently, "before he changes his mind."

Max took a step toward the room that led

to his own stairway, but Cecilia quickly laid a restraining hand on his arm and said softly, "No, don't go to your room yet. I need to talk to you. About Autumn."

"Is she sick?" Max asked in alarm, following her down the hall.

Cecilia lifted pain-filled eyes to Max's face. "She had another bad spell tonight. Her first in some time. And I know it was doubly hard on her because she had started hoping she might not really be terminally ill."

"Is she all right?" Max felt his heart plummet to his toes. He, too, had hoped desperately that Autumn's doctor was wrong.

"Yes, she's resting at last. But she was a pretty sick girl for awhile. That's how I happened to see Sherman come down here. I had been with Autumn and was just going back to my room when I saw him leave his room. He was acting so secretive, I knew he was up to something. There must be an alarm rigged up down there that went off when you entered."

As Max followed Autumn's mother through the large clean room, he wondered if she had suffered a mild stroke. She moved easily enough, but leaned heavily on the cane whenever she lifted her right leg.

She mounted the stairs, illuminated by small lights on the walls, ahead of him and pushed open the door.

As Max came out of the stairway, he saw they were in a small storeroom. Cecilia peeked out the door and then motioned him to come.

"We'll talk in my quarters," she said softly. "The things I want to talk to you about are private, and we'll not be disturbed there."

Max almost grinned. *I imagine I'm about to get another lecture about not getting involved with Autumn,* he thought wryly. *But I don't plan to desert her when she needs me.*

Pain filled his heart. He knew how much she would need a friend now; her hopes had been so high that her doctor's diagnosis was wrong. Poor Autumn!

Cecilia led the way into a room across the hall and pressed a switch to flood the room with light.

As Max moved to follow her inside, he thought he sensed a furtive movement down the hallway. Stopping abruptly, he looked that way but saw nothing.

Just jumpy, he thought, as he walked on into the room.

This was obviously a private suite. Max recognized the chandelier, suspended from the ceiling by a gold chain, as very old. The sparkling, candle-like bulbs glowed around a dainty arrangement of porcelain-like flowers of deep bougainvillea, interspersed with bright green leaves and vines. Although artificial, one could almost smell their fragrance.

Pale pink walls, polished beams overhead, the subdued glow of fine mesquite furniture and typically Mexican armchairs of carved wooden frames stretched with shiny cowhide charmed Max. The large curved sofa was heaped with colorful pillows. On a carved antique chest was a graceful blue ceramic vase filled with large paper flowers of every color in the rainbow.

"Please sit there on the sofa," Cecilia directed. "Would you like tea or coffee?" Cecilia asked. "They're both decaffeinated, I'm afraid. Caffeine affects me adversely."

Max objected to her providing anything for him this late at night, but she insisted with a gentle smile. "I'm making some tea for myself, so it's no bother. Besides, I have hot water ready, and the tea and coffee are both instant."

"Fine, then I'll have some tea, with sugar," Max said. "Can I help you?"

"No, I can manage quite nicely."

Cecilia moved to a small cubicle near the

wall that Max saw was furnished with a tiny refrigerator. The cabinet boasted a small work surface and a small glassed cupboard in which were arranged a few dishes and odds and ends of snack items. A stand on the counter held a gallon bottle of purified water. Taking two mugs from the cupboard, she measured tea into the cups.

Max had scarcely had time to seat himself on the sofa, it seemed, until she was placing a small silver tray on a small table set between the end of the sofa and a comfortable-looking armchair.

"I like a mug, if I'm having tea," she confided. "It stays hot so much longer." Handing one to Max, she set an identical one for herself on the other end of the table, next to the armchair. She placed a milk-white porcelain bowl filled with homemade cookies in the center of the small table.

"Could I have a glass of water, too, please?" Max asked. He laughed apologetically. "I guess all the excitement made me as dry as an Arizona sandstorm."

"Of course," Cecilia said. "I have some cold water in the refrigerator." She left for a few minutes and returned with a large glass of water which he drank thirstily.

Seating herself in the armchair, her cane at her feet, Cecilia took up her cup and sipped thoughtfully. Then setting the cup down carefully, she leaned toward Max, her face grave. "Now for our little talk."

Max could scarcely believe her next words. "I want to talk to you about God."

His surprise must have showed on his face because Cecilia laughed softly. "I suppose you're amazed that I would be interested in the things of the soul, but with cancer about to claim my daughter, I'm going to need help to — to live through it all."

"God is the place to go for help," Max said earnestly.

"I know. Autumn seems to have a new lease on life since she — she. . . ."

"Accepted Jesus Christ as her Savior," Max supplied gently.

"Yes, that's what she called it. Well, as you can see, I'm not very knowledgeable in the things of God. Autumn informed me that you were once a jewel thief, but that you gave your life over to God. He changed your life, and now you plan to train for the ministry."

"That's right." Max's face glowed and his amber eyes seemed to blaze with an inner fire. "God took the hate and evil from my life and replaced it with love and happiness like I didn't know existed. Knowing you are forgiven by God is the greatest experience possible in life," Max said huskily.

As Cecilia asked questions and listened attentively to his answers, Max explained salvation, marveling that it was so easy to talk to this sophisticated little woman. *I see where Autumn gets her charm,* he thought.

"Would you like some more tea?" Cecilia asked after a few minutes of conversation, noticing that Max's cup was empty.

"No, thank you, that's plenty," Max said.

"You make serving God seem very exciting and rewarding," Cecilia said. "I can't believe it is that easy."

"It isn't all easy, by any means," Max agreed. "I don't want to make it sound like a Christian never has any troubles, because he does. There are disappointments and heartaches for us Christians just like other people, but we have God to help us and others don't. Believe me, I have been on the other side of the fence, and I know what the Bible means when it says, 'the way of a transgressor is hard.' "

"You spoke of disappointments . . . ," Cecilia said, her eyes holding Max's with a burning intensity, though she spoke softly. "You are in love with my daughter. You know, of course, that she would never marry you."

Max felt his face grow scarlet, but he did

not drop his eyes and his voice was steady. "Yes, I love Autumn. She's a beautiful, sweet, caring person; the most wonderful lady I have ever met. And yes, I know she could never care for me as more than a friend, but I don't ask for more. If I can help to make her last days happy and maybe ease her pain somewhat, I'll feel my life has not been in vain."

A strange expression fleetingly crossed Cecilia's face. "Very noble," she said.

Was she being sarcastic? Before he had time to give it any more thought, she rose abruptly from the chair.

"Come let me show you something," she said enigmatically.

She crossed the room to a doorway and stood waiting for him, a strange half-smile on her aristocratic lips.

Mystified, Max arose and followed her to the door.

Cecilia opened the door. Grasping his arm firmly, she drew him into the room.

Max's eyes widened with shock; his heart leaped and then began to pound like a jackhammer.

Across the room, lying in a scarlet and cream velvet canopied bed was Autumn Caldwell! Her dark red hair was spread out in a flame of color on the creamy satin of her pillow. Her face was turned so he could see her lovely profile, serene in deep slumber. One shapely arm was curved about her face. A bright coverlet was pulled up around her shoulders. Her thin form barely lifting it.

Max tried to back from the room, but Cecilia tightened her fingers on his arm. "I just thought you would like to gaze upon the glorious Autumn for one last time."

A subtle change in her voice penetrated Max's confusion like a knife blade. "What do you mean, for one last time?"

Cecilia looked up at him, and her eyes had grown mocking, "Just what I said. Autumn is sleeping the sleep of death."

Max turned stunned eyes toward the bed. "What do you mean?" he demanded.

Cecilia didn't answer, so Max tore his arm from Cecilia's grasp and rushed to Autumn's side, calling urgently, "Autumn! Wake up! Wake up!"

The figure on the bed lay still and unmoving, except for the faint rise and fall of the coverlet.

"It's no use," Cecilia called from the doorway. "She will never speak again."

Slow, incredulous horror spread through Max. After one more glance at the wax-like figure on the bed, Max strode back to Cecilia. "What have you done to her?" he demanded harshly.

26

"Let's go back into Autumn's sitting room, and we'll talk about it," Cecilia said calmly. She moved aside for Max to precede her, then came out and drew the door almost closed.

"Please be seated again," she said in an emotionless voice.

Max did so, but his mind was in a turmoil.

Cecilia seated herself in the armchair and suddenly it struck Max. The cane was still lying near the chair. She had walked into the bedroom without using it — without even a limp!

"What are you?" Max demanded. "You don't need that cane you carry with you all the time! And you weren't really interested in hearing about God, were you?" Max hesitated. "And I have the feeling you're not the sweet motherly woman you appear to be!"

Cecilia suddenly laughed, a tiny tinkle of sound that somehow chilled Max to the core of his being.

"You're becoming very perceptive!"

"What have you done to Autumn?"

"She's heavily sedated." Cecilia laughed again, that eerie tinkle of mirthless sound. "When she discovers she has poisoned you — her latest conquest — she will be so devastated she will take an overdose of prescription drugs — or so it will appear to the world."

Max strove to calm his reeling senses. *Oh Father, help Autumn — and me,* he petitioned silently, as he said aloud, "In other words, you have given Autumn a lethal dose of sleeping pills — and you put poison in my tea." It was more a statement than a question.

"I'm afraid so, Max," Cecilia said gently, almost regretfully. "But you would not have had to die — with Autumn — if you had kept your nose out of our business. You were warned repeatedly to stay away from Autumn, but you persisted. So — I had no choice."

"And Autumn will be blamed for my murder, too, just as she was blamed for her husband's and the others." Max felt as if he were drowning, but he had to know the worst.

"Now, you're finally getting smart," Cecilia said disdainfully.

"How quickly will the poison work?"

"It is a slow acting poison, but sure. I

wanted to be certain Sherman is back in his bed asleep before you die. Then no one will ever suspect me."

"Why didn't you just let the dogs kill me?" Max asked angrily, "if you were going to murder me anyway."

Cecilia laughed softly. "Sherman unknowingly had a part in my play — and acted it out perfectly, I must say. But I couldn't let the dogs kill you. It must appear that our psychopathic Autumn did that."

Max rose and spoke angrily, "You're going to call Dr. Marler right now! If you don't, I'll. . . ."

"You'll do what?" Cecilia said, her fine lips curling with scorn. She drew her hand from her robe pocket, and the small, manicured fingers held a snub-nosed pistol. "I have time to wait," she said, "and so do you."

Max said slowly, "You wouldn't really pull that trigger."

"Oh, wouldn't I?" she said menacingly; her steady hand and cold blue-grey eyes upon him were very convincing.

"Sit back down and don't try to be a hero or Autumn will get the credit of shooting you rather than poisoning you. And the poison won't hurt like a bullet, I assure you!"

Max backed away and sat down.

Cecilia came nearer and took a seat in an ornate straight chair. Her hand held the gun steady and sure upon his heart.

She cocked her head and said conversationally, "Your being here is no accident, you know."

"What do you mean?"

She laughed condescendingly. "I was the one who invaded your bathroom tonight. I rattled some things around and then left quickly. I thought that even a chauffeur should be able to figure out where the opening to the basement was then."

"You have been in the basement before? You knew all along that Sherman has been dealing in drugs?" Max said slowly. "Of course! That's why the dogs knew you!"

"I always make it a point to know what's going on in my household! I have visited the dogs regularly — bringing them treats and lots of affection — ever since he brought them here. I didn't want to be torn to pieces if I needed to use the basement for any reason. I also knew where the alarm was so I could turn it off when I was in the basement."

"You're a real schemer, aren't you?" Max said dryly. "It would be my guess you killed Autumn's husband, too. Why did you do it?"

Cecilia's eyes sparked fire. "That pompous dictator thought he owned my daughter! She couldn't breathe unless he directed her how hard and how often.

"He treated us — her family — like we were on charity! *His* charity! He found out one day that I had filched some extra cash from my own daughter's safe, and he threatened to send us all packing. The miserable tightwad!"

"So you killed him."

Cecilia laughed as if the memory was pleasant. "I apologized profusely like a poor relative should and bided my time. A week later poison turned up in his nightly coffee.

"It was perfect timing. She and Royce had just had a bang-up fight that day! I put the poison in the coffee and of course the unsuspecting Autumn gave it to him.

"When Autumn realized Royce was dead, she went all to pieces. She couldn't even defend herself."

Cecilia's eyes sparkled and she lowered her voice conspiratorially, "After Dr. Marler gave her a heavy sedative, and she was sound asleep, I put the little poison bottle in her purse. The police didn't look farther than Autumn for the murderer.

"It helped when the servants remembered

the terrible argument Royce and Autumn had that day."

Max felt his flesh literally crawl. "What kind of woman are you that you could frame your own daughter and glory in her pain and anguish?"

Cecilia's eyes grew cold and a maniacal light glittered in them. "She was never a real daughter to me! She stole everything I ever cared for!"

"Like what?"

"Like my husband for starters! We were both actors in the theatre. We didn't get any great breaks, but we got along and had some successes. Warren admired me, and we celebrated each other's victories. Our careers and our love were enough for him — until she was born!

"Then he almost totally ignored Audra; even as a baby, she was plain and undemanding. But when Autumn was born, Warren took one look at her and exclaimed, 'She's beautiful! Look at that hair! Glorious! Like the red of autumn leaves. We'll call her Autumn and she's going to be the star of our family.'

"At first I was proud when people stopped me on the street to admire our lovely little girl. Autumn grew up and blossomed in the glow of adoring people. She had a natural grace and poise that drew people like a magnet."

Cecilia ground her small teeth together. "Warren recognized her 'uniqueness' — he called it — from the first. Before she could talk clearly, under his tutelage, she was doing commercials. He spent every penny we could rake together for music, singing, and drama lessons for her."

Cecilia's face twisted with hate. "The rest of the family — Sherman was here by then — might not have proper dental care, and we could wear thrift store cast-offs, but Autumn must have the best! She was going to make our fortune!"

Cecilia drew in a deep breath, and said bitterly, "And he was right! She did. The breaks came her way, and then, finally, Royce noticed her and agreed with Warren. Autumn was an actress with real potential! She was nineteen when he took her over and soon made her a star."

"You hated your husband, didn't you?" Max asked, trying to keep her talking. "You killed him, too, didn't you?"

Cecilia grimaced, as if in pain. "Warren began to compare Autumn and me. Soon, I could not come up to Autumn's level of perfection in anything. And he was always boasting that he had made her what she was.

"After her second enormous success, accompanied by rave reviews, he got drunk at the celebration and ridiculed me in front of our guests.

"It was too much! I was burning with anger at Autumn, too, because she had stolen Warren's affection. I recalled her pain and trauma when her teenaged boyfriend died in the boating accident so. . . ."

"So that was an accident?"

"Yes. The only thing Autumn can't do well is swim. She blamed herself because she was unable to help him and was a long time getting over it."

"You wanted Autumn to suffer — so you killed her father in her room! How vicious can a person get?" Max said, his eyes filled with wrath.

But his anger seemed to have no effect on Cecilia. She continued as if she hadn't heard him.

"Warren was staggering drunk, so I lured him into Autumn's room after she was asleep. I opened the window and pretended to show him an accident out in the street below our sixth story apartment. When he leaned out, I hit him over the head with this pistol — he had given it to me for protection soon after we married. I was small, but strong, then, because of my dancing. I pushed him out the window and quickly went back to my room."

"And you killed Autumn's doctor, too, didn't you?"

"Yes! He wanted Autumn to marry him, and I had already been through one husband of hers who tried to kick us out. I had to kill him to insure our income. And I forced Dr. Marler into helping me."

Her eyes glittered. "Dr. Marler is my first cousin, and I had asked him to live with us long before. It was nice to have a free doctor in the house. But his health had begun to fail, he had made a bad mistake that could easily have finished his medical career, so I threatened to throw him out of the luxury he had with us and cut off his allowance unless he helped me. He had no alternative but to help me."

She chuckled unpleasantly. "Now he's become so enmeshed that he is as guilty as I am!"

"You are a wicked woman!" Max said, aghast at her callousness. "How can you sleep at night?"

She tossed her head. "I learned a long time ago that there are weak people and there are strong people. The strong use the weak, and I determined to be strong! I have survived and will continue to do so!"

"There is also a God who sees everything you do!"

A hint of fear appeared in Cecilia's eyes briefly, then she lifted her chin haughtily. "Religion is for weaklings. Like I told you, I'm not weak!"

"What you think doesn't matter," Max said stubbornly. "God is watching you whether you believe in Him or not. And there will be a payday; if not here, in the hereafter."

Cecilia seemed to have forgotten the gun in her hand as she stared at him belligerently. It was no longer aimed at Max but rested on her knee.

Max kept his eyes on Cecilia's face but tensed to throw himself sideways while reaching for the gun. *Now!* he thought. But before he could put the command into action, Cecilia tightened her hold on the gun and again pointed it at his heart.

Cecilia laughed derisively. "So, you were about to play the hero! Remember, if you do, there will be a bullet in your heart before you get out of that chair! I'm a very good shot!"

Max relaxed his tensed muscles. He had to get the woman to talking again.

Heavenly Father, he cried out in his heart, *don't let this insane woman kill anymore! You are the only hope for Autumn and me.*

"How did you kill the other doctor?" Max asked. Not that he cared how she had done her crimes, but she seemed to enjoy talking about them — and he needed to keep her talking.

"Almost the same as before, only that time I got Laurence to help me throw him out the window. He was squeamish about it — the coward — but I insisted. I wasn't sure I could get his heavy body over the window sill. My husband was slim, but Dr. Reisner was a heavy man."

"I suppose you were also the one who pushed that big pot off on me."

Cecilia laughed softly. "Autumn almost caught me returning her dress and wig. I heard her coming from the bathroom and had to dash out. It's a good thing I'm still agile. I exercise every day — in the privacy of my room, of course. I can still do all my dance numbers as well as ever!"

"You're fit in every way . . . except in the mind," Max said. He locked his yellow eyes with Cecilia's and said harshly, "You're insane, you know."

Black fury raged in Cecilia's eyes. Leaping up, she aimed the gun at his head. "That's not true! I'm as sane as anyone! I have a good mind to fill you full of bullets!"

Max continued to look steadily into her eyes, trying to not betray the quivering of his stomach.

After a moment, the maniacal fire went out of Cecilia's eyes and she sat down, lowering her gun to his middle.

"You almost goaded me into shooting you. But the noise might bring some of the family, and I wouldn't want that. Of course, if I have to shoot you, I'll just tell them you came in on Autumn, and I had to shoot you."

"Which would be another of your lies!"

The voice caused Cecilia to start. She jumped up but kept the gun trained on Max.

Audra — dressed in a long, blue bathrobe — stood just inside the door. Her plain face was white and drawn but her blue-grey eyes were spitting fire.

"How long have you been standing there?" Cecilia demanded.

"Long enough to hear that my own mother has killed three times and is about to kill two more people — one her own daughter!" Audra's voice shook, and she caught her lower lip between her teeth to still its trembling and then rushed on.

"What kind of mother would cause her daughter so much pain and grief? Think of what you have put Autumn through! Your own child! And she has never done anything but good to you!"

"That's enough!" Cecilia ordered. Her face had gone ashy white when Audra entered. She seemed to age before Max's very eyes, until she looked haggard and old. Obviously, what Audra thought of her meant a great deal to Cecilia.

Cecilia's voice dropped and she said in a wheedling voice, "Please try to understand, Audra. Autumn took everything from me: my husband's love, my self-respect." Her eyes kindled, "I had to take *her* charity!

"If I could have had the teachers she had, I might have become an even greater actress than she was. But Warren insisted everything had to be spent on her!"

Cecilia's voice was beseeching. "You — of all people — should understand, Audra. You were cast aside, too, and never had the money or teachers to develop your talent."

The fire went out of Audra's eyes, and she stood mutely while her mother continued in a rush of breathless words, "But it isn't too late for us, Audra. We will finally have Autumn's money — all of it, not just an allowance — to hire good teachers and the best agents. You and I can still rise to the top. Don't you see that I'm doing this for you —

and Sherman — as well as for myself."

Audra's eyes were pitying. "I have hated Autumn at times, and I gave her a terrible time when we were growing up. But I never let hate warp me to the place that I would kill or condone killing!"

She swallowed hard and said gently, "Give me the gun, Mother. There's been enough killing."

Cecilia shook her head slowly and then more vigorously. "No — no! I've planned this for a long time, and I won't be stopped now. If this meddling chauffeur," she glared at Max and then returned her gaze to Audra, "hadn't shown up when he did, Autumn would be dead already! And I would never have to beg for the crumbs from her table again!"

"She's going to die anyway, Mother. So why must you hasten her death? At least let her live in peace for the time she has left!"

A strange expression flitted over Cecilia's face, and she said softly, "But she will never suffer again, Audra. Don't you see? I am really doing her a favor. It would be a mercy to her not to know the inevitable pain."

Max spoke up quietly. "I believe if another doctor checked Autumn, he would find that she doesn't have cancer at all. Isn't that so, Mrs. Cassel?"

Audra turned startled eyes to Max.

"That's why your mother has to kill her now — before another doctor examines her and confirms what I suspect: that Autumn is not sick at all but is being slowly poisoned to death. And she has to get rid of me, too, because if Autumn dies, I'd have insisted on an investigation into her death."

Audra put her hand to her throat as if she were choking, and she looked at her mother with stricken eyes. "Is that true, Mother? Have you been poisoning Autumn?"

"Your doctor cousin has no doubt been helping," Max said harshly, when Cecilia seemed at a loss for words.

"And I don't want to die," said a clear voice nearby.

Cecilia's eyes grew wide with shock — and fear — as she looked up, and saw Autumn standing in her bedroom doorway.

Cecilia's whole body seemed to sag as she stared at Autumn, and Max saw the opportunity he had been praying for. Like a tawny cat, he sprang forward and had his steel-like hands on Cecilia's wrists before she could recover from the shock of Autumn's sudden appearance.

Letting out one piercing shriek, Cecilia fought to free her hands and to bring the gun up, fighting him with all the power in her small, agile body.

But Max's hands were like steel traps, and she was at his mercy. Keeping the gun pointed at the floor, he continued to put pressure on her wrists until, with a moan, she dropped the gun.

Max kicked it toward Autumn who quickly grabbed it. Releasing Cecilia's wrists, Max tried to back away but she leaped at him, screaming vile names and tearing at his face with her nails.

Audra came up quickly from behind and grasped her mother's wrists, trying to draw her away from Max, but she turned on

Audra, kicking and screaming with fury. Together, Max and Audra finally managed to push her into an armchair. She subsided for a minute until she could get her breath, and then she lashed out at Max, "You're still going to die! The poison in your system is going to kill you!"

"Dear God, help us! I forgot about the poison!" Max said. Turning to Audra and Autumn, he said urgently, "Get your doctor up here quick. I'm not going to die, your mother is, unless we get help for her immediately."

Cecilia looked like she was going to faint. "W-what do you mean?" she asked in a strangled voice.

"I thought it strange that you were suddenly so friendly with me, and that those dogs seemed to know you, so I switched our tea cups — just in case you were up to mischief."

Cecilia stared at him for a moment — horror vivid on her haggard face. Then she crumpled and began to cry — great heart-rending sobs of utter defeat. "And to think I used to stand in Autumn's room after she was asleep and dream of the time when she would be dead and out of my life. Now it is never to be!" She seemed almost unaware of the others in the room as she sobbed out her despair.

Autumn snatched up the intercom and punched a button. As she waited, she told Max, "It's a good thing I put this in when I got sick. It's a direct line to Dr. Marler's room.

"Laurence," Autumn spoke into the intercom, "come quickly! It's an emergency. Mother accidentally took poison. . . . Yes — yes, the one she meant for Max. Please come quickly and pump out her stomach or something!"

Autumn sank down in a chair. "He's coming." Her lovely face was pale, but otherwise she seemed all right.

"How did you wake up so soon?" Max asked. "Your mother said you would never wake up. And you appeared to be sleeping deeply when she took me in there a short while ago."

Autumn smiled wanly. "I was never asleep at all. I suspected something when Juana brought me a tray and said no one felt like eating formally tonight. I got to thinking that if anyone meant to harm me it would be tonight — before I went to another doctor. So I dumped the food and milk in the toilet and just pretended to be asleep. When mother brought you into my room, I knew she was up to something so I pretended to be asleep so I could learn what.

"I didn't know if anyone really meant to harm me, but I took a gun to bed with me just in case!"

"You heard all your mother told me?"

"Yes, and I was so scared for you, but I didn't dare come out for fear she would shoot you. Then, when Audra came in, I didn't think she would shoot all of us. Beside, she always loved Audra."

Audra looked as if she were very ill, white and drawn, "Autumn," she sad tremulously, "what-what are we going to do — about mother? She's a cold-blooded murderer . . . but she is our mother."

The doctor arrived at that moment with his medical bag. He came over and looked at the still sobbing woman, then shook his head. "There's nothing I can do," he said, "it's been too long."

Cecilia raised an anguished, tear-wet face. "That isn't true and you know it, Laurence! Don't you want me to live?"

The doctor looked at Cecilia for a long moment, then spoke matter-of-factly. "No, Cecilia, I don't. You have ruined the lives of everyone around you and murdered the rest. I would do this world a favor to let you die and I plan to." He turned away.

Cecilia cried out, "Laurence! That would be murder! Murdering your own cousin!"

The doctor turned back to Cecilia and spoke wonderingly, "You condemn *me*, when for months you have been poisoning your own daughter!"

He shifted his gaze to Autumn. "I don't know how I ever let myself be drawn into this woman's web. She's as vicious and heartless as the black widow spider Sherman accuses you of being! It would have been far better for me to be in the poor-house than to have been a party to such evil. And the horrors this woman dreamed up have steadily gotten worse."

"Laurence, save her life!" Autumn pled. "Please. . . ."

"No, I will not!" he said, walking toward the door.

Audra ran after him and caught his arm, but he shook her off. "By the way, Autumn," his voice sounded tired as he turned back, "there's no need to see another doctor. You do not have cancer." He went out the door without another backward look.

Cecilia began to cry again, great heart-broken sobs.

Max went to her and shook her arm to get her attention, "Isn't there time to get an-other doctor?"

Numbly, she shook her head. "No, I can

feel the poison now. I doubt he could have saved me anyway."

Suddenly she seemed to come out of her self-pitying stupor and said angrily to Max, "You killed me! If you had told me right away that you had tricked me, there would have been time to get another doctor."

"And you would have shot me and killed Autumn, too," Max said. "I didn't dare tell you until I had the gun."

With Autumn's permission, Max called Dr. Otero. Audra went to get Sherman, but was soon back with the news that he refused to come. "He said he was afraid of death and didn't have the nerve to see Mother die," she said.

While waiting for the doctor, Max tried to talk to Cecilia about accepting Christ, but she only swore at him. Autumn sat down beside her and with tears running down her pale face — told her she forgave her. Cecilia turned her face away and said spitefully that she didn't need or want her forgiveness.

She wouldn't even let Audra near her, accusing her of taking sides with Autumn.

Shortly before Dr. Otero arrived, Cecilia Cassel died as she had lived — a bitter woman full of hate and malignancy.

28

Early one morning, almost a month after Cecilia's death, Max walked out onto the flagstone paving outside his rooms and stretched his muscular arms lazily over his tawny head. Ambling down the walk, his steps turned of their own volition toward the high iron grilling of the divider wall.

Every morning since the traumatic night of Cecilia's death, Max had gone to the gate and stood for a few minutes. Autumn had left as soon as the police had departed that morning.

When Dr. Marler had left Cecilia's room after refusing to help her, he had locked himself into his room. When the police came, they had tried to get him to open the door, but their appeals were answered with complete silence.

Audra had produced a key for the door and when it was opened, they had found him — head on his desk — dead from an overdose of sleeping pills.

But before he died, Dr. Marler had written down a record for the family — and for the courts of law — a precise and lucid account of the murders Cecilia had perpetrated, and of the part he and she had played in the killings. The record also gave a full report of Cecilia's attempt to murder Autumn and Max.

He urged that the public be fully informed about the defaming of Autumn's character and that the whole story be made public so she could return to the States — and to her acting career, if she so desired.

Max had seen Autumn — pale and hollow-eyed with grief — briefly before she had gone back to the States, taking the bodies of her mother and Dr. Marler for burial.

When Max had asked if she was returning to Mexico City, Autumn had been vague.

"This whole affair has been a horrendous nightmare," she said. "I can't even think straight yet. But I will contact you later and let you know what I plan to do."

She had smiled sadly, "Even the fact that I am not dying doesn't seem real."

Her voice had quivered as she reached up and touched him lightly on the cheek with her lips. "Dear, dear Max, you are the dearest friend a girl ever had. I thank God every day for you."

Then she had left, and there had been no word of any kind. At first Max had watched the house next door eagerly, expecting her momentary return. And when the phone rang, his heart leaped in anticipation. But he had heard nothing.

Skye and Joy had watched him anxiously, suffering with him.

"Max, get involved with some work down at the church," Skye urged. "If you want to take off a week or so, we can spare you. Try to get your mind off of Autumn.

"Remember, Max, she has thought for a long time that she was dying. I'm sure she feels like she has been born again — in a different way now."

Joy chimed in, "And since her name has been cleared, I'm sure the public will be clamoring to make up to her what her mother tried to take away. People love a sensational story, and now she will be more popular than ever before."

Max looked at both of them, then said gravely, "You don't think she'll ever contact me again, do you?"

"You have to admit she has been gone a long time without a word," Joy said gently. "She is a wonderful woman, but with all those people swarming around her and making over her, she may mean to call or write you — but she has put it off. Time passes quickly."

"I know," Max said miserably. "I'll try to get involved with the kids down at the church — maybe tomorrow. And thanks for your concern."

He did go down to the church one day and volunteered to help on a project with the local children, but he couldn't throw himself into it. His thoughts were back at the house — afraid she would come back or call and he wouldn't be there. So he had given it up and gone home, his heart anxious.

But Autumn's house had remained deathly still except for the swish of Jorge's machete on the expanse of grass surrounding the *ramada*.

Joy and Skye's two lively youngsters had arrived with their grandparents, and that had helped to pass the long days. Max was kept busy chauffeuring everyone around, sightseeing and shopping. The evening meals were festive affairs — often with friends invited — and Max was in charge of these.

Trying to keep his mind blanked out during the busy days — but not always succeeding — Max had seen the minutes creep by with no word from Autumn. The nights were harder. Often, he had to pray for a long while before he could sleep.

This morning Max walked to the divider gate and looked through the iron grillwork toward the gazebo. As usual, it was empty, but his mind drifted back to weeks before when he had first seen Autumn lying on the steps, her dark flame-colored hair spilling out, her face pale and white.

Now the whole world was at her feet again. Her health had been restored, and with plenty of money, she could live anywhere and do anything she chose to do. She could again be a great theater star.

And he — Max Parrish — would be going away to mission school soon, working hard at learning the Bible, Spanish, and carpentry. And working harder yet at trying to forget the beauty, charm, and sweetness of a woman named Autumn Caldwell!

Max sighed deeply. With God's help, he would, no doubt, be able to put Autumn on a treasured shelf in his mind, and pick up the tattered threads of his heart. He might not even miss her — someday. But at the present, the world looked bleak, indeed.

He turned around to go back to the house.

"Hi, Max!"

His heart seemed to stop beating. It

couldn't be — but it was! He spun around. Autumn, a large white hat swinging in one slim hand, was running lightly across the patio toward him.

Max could never remember opening the gate, but in a moment, he was standing in its opening watching her approach.

His eager eyes swept over her and saw that her coloring had deepened, the circles under her sparkling blue-grey eyes were gone, and her oval face had filled out. It glowed with health and vitality.

Autumn came quickly to Max, holding out her hand, almost shyly, it seemed to him. "How are you, Max?"

It took two tries before he got out a word. To his chagrin, he gulped like a moonstruck teenager and finally managed, "I'm fine."

He had forgotten how beautiful Autumn really was and despair engulfed him. Seeing her, he knew he loved this lovely, much-sought-after woman — with all his heart! He had tried to focus only on their friendship in the last four weeks. But he was hopelessly, totally in love, even though he acknowledged the impossibilities of that love.

"You look so serious — and solemn, Max," she said softly. "I had thought you might be glad to see me."

"I am! I've been looking for you all

month," Max blurted out, then quickly added, "Not that you were obligated to call — or anything."

"Do you have time to chat for a bit?" Autumn asked. When he assured her he did, she walked with him to the gazebo.

"I intended to call," she said apologetically, "but things were so hectic, I could hardly keep up with everything.

"There were the arrangements for both funerals, all kinds of business connected with my estate, and the press followed us everywhere we went. That part was a pain! And to think there was a time when I enjoyed that sort of thing!"

As they climbed the steps, she rested her slim hand on his arm for balance and Max rebuked his foolish heart soundly when it started banging away joyously beneath his ribs at her touch.

"I arrived late last night. Juana is bringing breakfast out here to the gazebo. I hope you haven't already eaten."

Max admitted he had not. "Are you all right now?" Max asked. "Are you getting over the shock of your mother — and all?"

Autumn looked down at her hands folded loosely together on the table. "No. It will take a long time for me to completely recover from the feelings I'm struggling with."

She looked up at Max, and tears suddenly trembled on her dark eyelashes. "Max, I think it hurt me worse than anything to know mother had rejected me. It was even worse than the shock of knowing she was methodically poisoning me."

She shuddered. "I know it was God who intervened or I — and you — would have been dead for almost a month now . . . instead of her."

She reached out and laid her hand on Max's arm. "Max," she said softly, "I have thanked God every day, since I came to know Him, for you! If you had not come, and cared enough to tell me about Christ, I would not only be dead but I would never have known His joy and peace."

Embarrassed, Max shook his head emphatically. "I was just used by God for this part of His plan."

His heart felt warm and almost happy again. Even though he could never share his life with Autumn, he would always have the joy of knowing he had been the vessel used by God to bring her to Him. His heart leaped with joy at the thought.

Juana appeared with a bountiful breakfast and Max, who had not cared for food lately, suddenly discovered he was very hungry.

"How does it feel to know you are not

really sick?" Max asked softly.

A glad light flared in Autumn's eyes. "Marvelous! Whenever things got to be more than I could handle, I'd remind myself that I wasn't dying, and everything seemed brighter right on the spot!"

"Did Roycie and Audra come back with you?"

"They'll be here next week. Roycie's grandmother wanted to keep him for another week since Audra was delayed for a week."

"Is Sherman coming back?"

"Absolutely not! He had quite a scare before we went back to the States for the funeral. When he called his drug partners and told them that he wanted out of the deal, they didn't say much. But when we got to the airport, that Mexican, with the gold ring in his ear, cornered Sherman in the restroom and pulled a knife on him. Sherman barely got away and was so shaken that he swears he'll never come back to Mexico City.

"I told him that I would help him get settled in a job or send him to school, but I did not plan to continue supporting him. He's decided to open a kennel and dog obedience school. I promised to loan him the money to get the business going on one condition: he

315

couldn't raise pit bulls. He agreed."

Autumn smiled. "Do you know, Max, Sherman is actually as excited as a kid about his kennel and school. It's exciting to see it. I didn't know that Sherman loves dogs and has a real knack for training them."

"I know that takes a lot of worry off you."

"Yes, it does. He really did care about mother, and finding out that she murdered all those people almost destroyed him. He never apologized to me about the things he said about me and to me, but he is no longer sarcastic to me and even treats me with a little respect."

"How are things between you and Audra?"

Autumn's eyes sparkled. "There has always been the jealousy I mentioned between us. But we have had several wonderful talks and literally bared our souls to each other. We are learning to talk to each other — really talk."

A lilt came into her voice. "I think I have gained a sister out of this mess! I begged her to stay with me and told her how much I appreciated how she has been a mother to Roycie when I was not, and that I need her as a sister, not as hired help to mother my child.

"Also, I assured her that I had never felt

that she was living on my charity. I'm so sorry I was so blind to the possibility. I never knew mother was bothered by it." Sadness filled her voice for a moment. Then she continued, "Audra objected, but I set a plan in motion to put some of my holdings in her name, no strings attached. After all, I owe her so much for caring for Roycie. This way, she can be free to live her life any way she chooses. When she saw I was sincere, she accepted my gift graciously, and even threw her arms around me and kissed me. We both cried a little."

Max reached across and took one of Autumn's hands in his large ones and said huskily, "You are a wonderful person, Autumn. I also thank God every day that I met you."

Abruptly, he realized that he was holding Autumn's hand and drew his hands back quickly. He could feel his face grow hot, and he felt like a fool.

He grabbed his coffee cup and put it to his lips, to hide his confusion and embarrassment.

When he dared raise his eyes to Autumn's face, he saw her regarding him intently. Her lips were curved in a little smile, and amusement danced in her eyes.

Max looked down at his plate, afraid that she was laughing at him. She must have read how he felt about her in his face. He was never very good at hiding his feelings.

Well, let her laugh! Maybe if she did, he would get over his feelings for her!

He braved another glance at her face and saw her still looking at him. Only her face was now very grave.

Suddenly, Autumn reached across and took one of Max's hands in her two cool, soft hands. She ran her fingers lightly across his palm and then looked up at him. "I like your hands, Max. They're the hands of a real man. A man who has become very special to me."

Her voice was low, and it trembled slightly. "I heard you tell mother that you loved me. Did you really mean that, Max?"

Max felt the color surge into his face again, and the pounding of his heart seemed to shake his body but he answered honestly, "Yes. I think I've loved you from the first minute I saw you."

"And I love you," Autumn said simply.

For an incredulous moment, tremendous joy exploded in Max's big chest. Then reason took over. Autumn did not mean the same kind of love he felt for her. This beautiful woman could never love him: an ex-con, scarred face, and built like a bulldog! She must be saying this out of gratitude to him. After all, gratitude was a form of love.

"It's kind of you to say that," he said, gently withdrawing his hand.

Sudden pink rose in her cheeks. "Max Parrish, I have all but proposed to you and you brush me off like a fly!"

Max stared at her in confusion and then blurted out miserably, "Please don't toy with me, Autumn. I care about you deeply — and not the gratitude kind that you feel for me. I told your mother I didn't expect you to love me in return, and I don't!"

He tried to laugh lightly but it came out harsh and bitter. "With a face like mine, not to mention my past, I knew a beautiful, talented, wealthy woman could never love me. I. . . ."

"Max," Autumn interrupted, "I have been surrounded with handsome men all my life. Father, Royce, and the leading men I acted with in the theater were all handsome. But none of them had the qualities that count — the qualities you have."

Her blue-grey eyes misted, "You are beautiful to me, Max, because you are beautiful inside."

Max's voice was tender. "You're sweet, Autumn. I feel honored that you care for me as a friend." He drew in a ragged breath, "And I hope we can always be friends."

Suddenly Autumn began to laugh, at first a nervous sort of titter and then uproariously, until tears ran down her cheeks.

Max stared at her, first perplexed and then hurt.

As suddenly as she had begun, Autumn stopped laughing. Wiping her wet eyes with a napkin, she stood to her feet. Before the startled Max could move, she came around the table. Bending down, she put her hands on his shoulders and said gently, "It seems there is only one way to prove that I love you . . . as much more than a friend."

She laid her warm, petal-soft lips on his.

For a moment, Max was too stunned to move. Then he stood hastily to his feet, took Autumn in his arms and answered her kiss with a message of his own.

29

Emilia had just placed breakfast on the table for Skye and Joy when Max came into the dining room.

"Come on over and have some breakfast with us," Skye invited. "Or has the early bird already eaten?"

Before Max could answer, Joy exclaimed, "Max! Something has happened to you! Your face is glowing!"

"Autumn has come back!" Skye declared. "That's the only thing that would make Max look like he swallowed a thousand watt bulb."

"Has she?" Joy asked. "Come on, Max, don't stall. I'm dying of curiosity."

Max sat down at the table and looked at first one and then the other.

"Yes, Autumn came in last night," he said, "and she plans to make Mexico her home."

He smiled. "Autumn has decided to start Bible school in the fall. When she graduates, she wants to teach."

"That's fantastic!" Skye said. "With her

magnetism, she will be a dynamic teacher."

"We plan to teach as a team," Max explained shyly. "After she becomes my wife."

"Max!" Joy jumped up, ran around the table, and hugged him.

When Joy returned to her chair, Skye stuck out his hand, "Congratulations are in order, it seems." A slight frown creased his brow. "I'm always the old killjoy, but you aren't jumping into things too quickly, are you, Max?"

Max shook his head emphatically. "No. We don't plan to marry right away. Autumn needs time to get her feet back on the ground after her mother's death and all.

"There is no doubt in my mind about what I feel for Autumn, but I want to give her space so she is sure — really sure — about her feelings for me. She says she is as sure as I am, but agrees that it is wise to not rush into things."

He suddenly grinned like a bashful kid. "Besides, I don't want to miss out on courting Autumn proper!"

He gazed at them in wonder. "I still can't believe a gorgeous girl like Autumn could fall in love with a lug like me."

"Well, I can believe it!" Joy said stoutly. "She couldn't find a finer man anywhere!"

Max smiled his thanks, then said seriously, "Autumn said that when we went to the Mexican church and had lunch with the pastor's family, she fell in love with the people she met. She felt a strong desire to really get to know them and to work with them, not even dreaming she would be alive to do it. Her dream is to teach music and singing — and maybe even drama — in Bible school."

Max's face was transformed by the joy that radiated from it as he continued in a serious voice, "I know God has called me to be a missionary. I plan to enroll in Bible school in the fall, too. I can hardly wait."

"We'll be praying for you," Skye said with a catch in his voice. "Even if it does mean we're losing the best chauffeur and personal assistant we ever had."

Max fell silent for a moment and then said musingly, "Roycie told me a while back that he wished I were his dad." His lips suddenly curved into a broad grin, "You know, I think I'll make a good papa!"

The employees of Thorndike Press hope you have enjoyed this Large Print book. All our Thorndike and Wheeler Large Print titles are designed for easy reading, and all our books are made to last. Other Thorndike Press Large Print books are available at your library, through selected bookstores, or directly from us.

For information about titles, please call:

(800) 223-1244

or visit our Web site at:

www.gale.com/thorndike
www.gale.com/wheeler

To share your comments, please write:

Publisher
Thorndike Press
295 Kennedy Memorial Drive
Waterville, ME   04901